PRAISE FOR

The Silence of John

"Outstanding . . . Highly recommended."
—*Library Journal* (starred review)

"Lliteras sees in them [women] the best
humankind has to offer."
—*Booklist*

"*The Silence of John* explores the loyalty and sacrifice
of Jesus' female disciples, John's helplessness, and
the cultural exclusion of women at that time."
—*Publishers Weekly*

"*The Silence of John* is a fabulous entry in a
terrific [and] insightful series."
—*Midwest Book Review*

PRAISE FOR

Judas the Gentile

"Top 10 Christian Novel of 2000.
Subtle, provocative."
—*Booklist* (starred review)

"Judas' struggle to understand his motives, his
faith and his destiny propel the tale."
—*Publishers Weekly*

"D. S. Lliteras has given readers much to
think about in *Judas the Gentile*."
—*Midwest Book Review*

"A true work of enduring literature . . ."
—*Wisconsin Bookwatch*

"Enormously rewarding."
—*The Virginian-Pilot*

"*Judas the Gentile* is so honest and
elemental that it seems like the truth."
—*Christian Fiction, A Guide to the Genre* (starred review)

PRAISE FOR

The Thieves of Golgotha

"Startling, surprisingly successful . . ."
—*Booklist*

"Thought-provoking . . . Recommended."
—*Library Journal*

"A sympathetic fictional portrait."
—*Publishers Weekly*

"A tough, vivid, extraordinary novel."
—*Christian Fiction, A Guide to the Genre* (starred review)

The MASTER *of* SECRETS

a novel

D. S. LLITERAS

HAMPTON ROADS
PUBLISHING COMPANY, INC.
for the evolving human spirit

Also by D. S. Lliteras:

The Silence of John

Jerusalem's Rain

Judas the Gentile

The Thieves of Golgotha

613 West Jefferson

In a Warrior's Romance

In the Heart of Things

Into the Ashes

Half Hidden by Twilight

I will give you treasures
concealed in the darkness.
—Isaiah 45:3

A true mystic is always prepared to
be in a state of spiritual crisis.
—DSL

God called out to the
man, "Where are you?"
—Genesis 3:9

Cover design by Frame25 Productions
Cover art by Sarah Johnson c/o Shutterstock
Typesetter: Frame25 Productions

Hampton Roads Publishing Company, Inc.
1125 Stoney Ridge Road
Charlottesville, VA 22902
phone: 434-296-2772 • fax: 434-296-5096
e-mail: hrpc@hrpub.com • www.hrpub.com

If you are unable to order this book from your local
bookseller, you may order directly from the publisher.
Call 1-800-766-8009, toll-free.

Library of Congress Cataloging-in-Publication Data

Lliteras, D. S.
  The master of secrets / D.S. Lliteras.
     p. cm.
  Summary: "D. S. Lliteras's latest novel follows Addan, a young
boy searching for his father, a disciple of Jesus. Along the way,
Addan encounters bandits, lepers, and con men before team-
ing up with Jeshua, an entertainer and opportunist, who
protects the boy while at the same time using him to help
swindle unsuspecting strangers"--Provided by publisher.
  ISBN 1-57174-538-6 (5 x 7.5 tc : alk. paper)
  1. Jesus Christ--Fiction. 2. Orphans--Fiction. 3. Swindlers
and swindling--Fiction. 4. Apostles--Fiction. I. Title.
  PS3562.L68M37 2007
  813'.54--dc22
                                        2006033710

ISBN 10: 1-57174-538-6
ISBN 13: 978-1-57174-538-5
10 9 8 7 6 5 4 3 2 1
Printed on acid-free paper in Canada

Dedicated to Kathleen Touchstone

TABLE OF CONTENTS

CHAPTER 1

Mother

The boy wanted his mother. But she was crying—like him. Like his sister. His brother. "Mother?"

She didn't hear him.

He waved his right hand to attract her attention, but tears prevented her from seeing him.

The boy trembled. He ran the palm of his left hand from his forehead to the back of his head, then down to the back of his neck. He gazed up at the cross and sought Jesus' tortured eyes. They were closed.

He lowered his gaze as his left arm fell to his side:

Who could hear or see anything after this?

"Jesus?" His whisper dissolved into an air that would not allow his off-key note of despair to reach its destination. "Jesus."

He reached for solace by extending his right arm into the farthest end of Jesus' shadow, but a woman stole the comfort he sought when she stepped into the shadow and unintentionally forced him to retract his arm.

The woman dropped to her knees, then leaned forward on her hands before she wept into the crucified shadow on the ground.

His mother turned to him, then acknowledged his existence before she approached him with a dangerous expression etched upon her stony face.

"Find your father." She grabbed his tunic by its left shoulder and pulled him toward her.

His eyes widened with confusion, which intensified her frenzy.

"Find your father." The furor in her hoarse whisper paralyzed him. "Go." She released his tunic as she pushed him away.

He staggered backward, slipped on the mud, and almost fell. When he regained his balance, he sought his mother's approval for reassurance, for love. "Mother?"

"Go," she whispered softly to convey the only reassurance he was going to get. She seemed ill. She turned away from him and peered at the head of the cross. "Go." There was no love woven into her distressed voice.

He backed away two steps before he was assaulted by continuous thunder and lightning that kept splitting the tormented sky after each pause in Jesus' Aramaic utterance: "Eloi, Eloi, why have you forsaken me?" Then lightning. "Eloi, into your hands I entrust my spirit." Then lightning. "Elah thirsts. It is finished." Then lightning. Followed by ordinary thunder and wind and rain.

The world became bigger and the wind blew more ferociously. Everything in the sky and on the ground seemed to be moving at the same time and, yet, everybody seemed to be afraid and unable to run away from where they stood. Women lamented upward at Jesus and wept from side to side at each other; they offered consolation when they bowed at their nervous children and tried to give comfort when they hovered over their crying babies. A multitude of anxious adolescent children orbited these Galilean women, these women of Jerusalem, these sister disciples, these midwives and mothers, these healers and prophetesses—the many unknown female figures that surrounded Jesus' crucified and lifeless body. The sobs of the women strangely complemented the elemental tumult of a black swirling sky and the chaotic colors of clothing that flapped and swirled in the wind. The colors mixed and bled into one another like one large smear on a painter's palate.

Cloaks and tunics and blankets fluttered in the wind. Some figures swayed. Others crouched. Some tried to bury their heads in their arms or in their outer garments or in their soggy mantles.

He saw everything separately, then altogether; he caught pieces of scenes here and there, here and now:

The world is coming to an end.

He wiped the tears from his face with the back of his right forearm then turned away from the bleak and frightening scene with a suddenness that caused him to stumble. He planted his right foot into the mud to prevent himself from falling, then firmly pivoted on his leg in order to direct himself away from the madness of his mother, away from the stillness of his Rabbi Jesus, and away from the plaintiveness of those who remained on Golgotha.

Ordinary fear was his source of motivation as he approached the outer darkness.

CHAPTER 2

Sister

The boy trembled within the gloom beyond the outer darkness. He grabbed the front of his tunic with his right hand and wrung the front of his garment.

He wore a dull, light brown woolen tunic that hung beltless below his knees; its sleeves came down to his forearms. The neck of the garment was split in the front about a palm's width in length—from the throat toward the chest. He wore hard leather sandals; their hide innersoles and straps were nailed to wooden soles. A dark-brown, beehive-styled woolen cap covered the back of his shaggy head and allowed his unruly black curls to sprout from underneath its entire circumference and cover the back of his neck as well as frame his youthful face. He was short-legged and thin, narrow-chested but muscular.

His dark eyes and his broad masculine expressions compensated for his delicate facial features and his thin, adolescent voice.

The boy scanned the rugged region to penetrate the darkness. Gnarled olive trees were the dominant forms that sparsely dotted the black landscape. There must have been light from somewhere since there were shadows that helped define a stone wall to his left, a fallen tree to his right, the alignment of three olive trees ahead, which sparked an idea:

On the slopes of Mount Olivet—Gethsemane—that's where Rabbi Jesus had been arrested. That's where senior disciples and junior followers like his father had to have been. Yes. And maybe. Maybe some of them were still there. Maybe.

With the sudden orientation at having a destination, he lost some of his fear; he also became aware that he had passed through the outer darkness:

Somewhere. Back there.

Confusion replaced a portion of his remaining fear:

Where was . . . what was that outer darkness?

He turned around and searched for the line of darkness that surrounded—no—separated him from Golgotha:

Was the outer darkness over there? Or was it inside of him?

He shuddered. He shook away these notions, which he decided were too large for him to comprehend—even ponder:

His father. He had to find his father.

He took measured steps in the direction of Mount Olivet:

To his right. Toward the Hedron Valley. Mount Olivet. Gethsemane. He didn't know why he felt so pulled in this direction. Could it be that his father was actually still there?

A different kind of fear assaulted him:

If this were so, what was his father doing there? Why wouldn't he have been with—?

His growing anxiety forced him to pick up his pace despite the dangers created by the darkness. The ground he traveled on was fraught with chuckholes and ditches, rocks and ruts and slippery mud patches—obstacles, obscured by the gloom and waiting for him to make a careless step, a misstep, that would cause him to stumble and fall.

"Wait. Wait for me."

The shock of recognizing her voice stopped the boy from taking another step.

"Sister? Sister. What are you doing, my Sister?"

"I had to follow you."

"It's dangerous."

"Everywhere. It's dangerous, everywhere."

"You should be with Mother."

"She's no use. She's no comfort to anyone right now with her grief. She doesn't even know I've gone."

He studied his adolescent sister, who was the oldest among them.

She was strong and beautiful, intelligent and levelheaded. Her thick, dark hair peeked out from the front edge of her loosely draped mantle, which framed her lovely face composed of delicate features. His sister's nose was slight and pointed. Her face was uncommonly smooth and uniform.

His sister usually chose her words carefully and walked obediently. Her dark eyes pierced into the things that adults called the truth. Her intelligence confused him sometimes, but her unwavering devotion always balanced his confusion with trust.

He trusted her completely. But he was the firstborn son, and he was only one year younger than she. So, his words had greater weight, and his presence was, at times, less invisible within the family circle. Of course, outside this sphere, he was as invisible as any boy or girl or woman.

He peered at his sister without judgmental eyes, hoping to avoid an argument. "You should be looking after our younger brother and sister. You're the eldest among us."

"They're your brother and sister too."

It began to rain heavily. She sheltered her eyes with the palm of her left hand pressed perpendicularly against her forehead.

"You should take Mother's place right now," he cautiously suggested.

She clenched her teeth to prevent herself from snapping at her brother. "I know they are being looked after."

"I'm sorry."

"You should know me better than that."

"I said I'm sorry."

"They are being cared for."

"I won't apologize again."

"I'm going with you."

"But—"

"I'm going."

He clenched his teeth. "Mother needs you. You're the only one that exists for her right now."

"I don't care."

"You must. Father might be dead. And . . . and she needs your strength."

"And if he's not dead?"

He turned his back toward the angle of the rain then wiped the rain from his burning eyes with his hands. "Then I'll need to have strength. So I can't have you around making me feel less than myself than . . . than I am already when I'm with him."

"It's not my fault you lose your confidence. You do that to yourself. You're the one who is afraid of Father."

"So are you."

"That's expected of me."

"Yes. Well. I'm . . . I'm not—"

"Please. Let me come with you."

"Please, Sister. Please. Stay with the women and children. I need you to be there. I need your eyes there as much as you need my eyes to find whatever I've been instructed to find by Mother." He approached her and placed a gentle hand on her right shoulder. "We must support each other. We must."

She faltered. "Yes."

"You take care of Mother. And I'll . . . I'll be with Father, if I can find him." He squeezed her shoulder for emphasis. "And, I swear, I'll share everything I witness with you." He released her shoulder. "You can do the same for me." He cocked his head to the right and peered intently into her eyes. "Please?"

She exhaled. "All right. All right. But be careful."

"No. You—you be careful." He tried to peer through Golgotha's outer darkness. "You must penetrate that darkness before it lifts."

"If it ever does."

"It will. Don't ask me how I know." He bit his lower lip. "But you must go now while it is still safe to do so."

"You're frightening me."

"Go back, Sister." He kissed her on the cheek. "Hurry. Please."

"Be careful, Brother." She kissed him. "Do not be too zealous over your duty as a son."

He grinned. "Nor you as a daughter."

She nodded. "I promise." Their warm exchange calmed her. She adjusted the top of her soaked mantle past her forehead to protect her eyes from the rain, then flung the lower right portion of her mantle across her left shoulder to cover the lower portion of her face. "Be careful."

He nodded respectfully. "Go."

She turned from him, took a reluctant step, then proceeded into the outer darkness with a steadily growing determination.

"Be careful," he whispered, to himself. "Be careful, my dearest sister."

CHAPTER 3

Brigands

The rain intensified and the sky rumbled. The boy splashed through the standing water at a trot.

He stopped to catch his breath. He shivered with uncertainty. His mud-stained tunic clung heavily to his skin. His sandaled feet were immersed ankle deep in muddy water.

He searched for a horizon.

Thunder rumbled in the distance. The darkness flickered from lightning striking another region. There were no stars.

He heard hostile voices. Hard friendless voices. He squinted into the darkness and saw several figures approaching him.

He ran in the opposite direction. The splash of his feet drew their attention.

"Over there! After him!"

He traveled a short distance before one of his pursuers grabbed his tunic from behind and yanked him off his feet. He splashed into the mud, onto his rump.

"I've got him!" The man held the boy upright by the back of his tunic. Two other men approached him.

"Is that him?"

"I don't know." The man pulled the boy to his feet. "Wait. No. This can't be him."

One of the other men leaned close to the boy. "Who are you? Talk. Or I'll slit your throat."

"I'm . . . I'm nobody. Son of—"

"It's a boy!"

"Uncover your lamp."

"Are you crazy?"

"Uncover it! There's nobody out here who would dare challenge us."

The man uncovered the lamp and released a feeble glow that illuminated the face of the brutish man who held the boy captive. He had a terrible scar cut diagonally across his entire face.

The man with the lamp shielded the flame with one of his hands to protect it from the wind and rain. He was a thin, mean-looking character who had a ragged piece of cloth wrapped and tied around his head.

The third man stepped between the boy's captor and the lamp holder. "What have we got?" He squatted inside the light. He wore a filthy sackcloth tunic gathered at the waist by a length of rope. "Shine the light on him, not me." The man was toothless and as scraggly bearded as his companions.

The lamp emitted enough light for the boy to see that all the men were dressed raggedly.

The man with the lamp guided the struggling flame closer for inspection. "You're right. It is a boy."

"Ha! A small fish," said the toothless man.

"Hooked nonetheless," said the man with the scar.

The man with the lamp studied him. "What are you doing out here, boy?"

"And why were you running?" the man with the scar prodded.

"I . . . I was running from you."

The scar-faced man who held the boy by his tunic slapped him across the back of his head. "Don't be smart with us, boy."

"What are you doing out here?" the man with the lamp repeated.

"I'm . . . I'm looking for . . . for my father."

"And who would that be?" the scar-faced brute demanded.

"Nobody you'd know."

"I told you don't get smart, boy."

"A follower of Jesus and . . . and of Simon Bar-Jona of Bethsaida."

"Who?"

"Simon—"

"Oh. You mean Kephas," said the man who held the lamp.

The scar-faced brute snickered. "You mean, that big fool who thinks he's in charge of Jesus' band of disciples."

"Yes," said the lamp holder. "That one."

"Simon. Kephas. Peter—whatever," the toothless man interjected. "They all refer to the same rock-head."

The scar-faced brute released a cruel chortle that originated from his belly. "Are you like him, boy? Are you? Are you?" He twisted the boy's tunic to increase the boy's discomfort. "He's the disciple who thought he was in charge of the others who followed Jesus of Nazareth throughout the countryside." The brutish man leaned closer to the boy with his bad breath. "Are you like one of those followers, boy?"

He trembled. "No. I mean, yes."

"No, yes—which one is it, boy?"

"Yes," he said, "yes, of course."

"Yes, of course," the scar-faced brute mimicked cruelly as he further tightened the grip he had on the boy's tunic to increase the pressure against his throat again. "Where is Judas? Do you know where he's hiding?"

"Judas? Hiding?"

The brute yanked hard on the tunic and choked him. "Don't pretend you don't know who he is, boy."

He gagged.

"Release the boy," said the lamp holder. He kicked the brute who kept choking him. "I said release the boy!"

He gasped and wheezed for breath as the man released him.

"Talk, boy."

"I . . . I don't . . . don't know where . . . where he is." He rubbed his throat with both hands. "I don't even know where my father is." He cleared his throat. "You didn't have to choke me."

"Shut up."

"All right, all right. Leave him alone. We've heard enough," said the toothless man. "He's one of us." He helped the boy to his feet. "Don't be frightened. We're not going to hurt you."

"He already has."

"Bah." The scar-faced brute spat on the ground. "You've had too much of your mother's milk, boy."

"Cover the lamp," ordered the toothless man.

Darkness equalized them.

The toothless man leaned closer to the boy. His breath smelled worse than the brute. "We're frightened, like you."

"Really?"

"And angry," said the scar-faced brute.

The boy straightened out his tunic. "Who are you? What kind of men are you?"

The man with the lamp chuckled. "We're—well—sometimes we're called bandits. Other times, brigands. We consider ourselves revolutionists."

"But Rome considers us criminals." The toothless man pressured the boy to respond. "Outlaws, boy. Outlaws."

"I don't really know anything about politics. I've . . . I've simply come from Golgotha where they've executed Rabbi Jesus—"

"And Azriel," the lamp holder interjected.

The toothless man grimaced. "Yes." He nodded at the boy as if this were common knowledge.

"Who?"

The toothless man punctuated his surprise with a grin. "This boy has no politics."

"Azriel, boy." The scar-faced brute nudged the boy's right shoulder to emphasize his impatience. "Azriel. He was one of the other two who were crucified with your Jesus."

"Yes," the toothless one added. "Rome had three of a kind in its hand. Who could wager against that?" He shook his head. "It was politically a clean sweep. Azriel. Poor Azriel. What a loss. He was a good man."

"Among bandits, you mean. Bandits against the power of Rome."

"Watch your tongue, little fish," said the scar-faced brute, "or I'll cut it out."

"Let him speak freely," said the lamp holder.

"He called us bandits."

"Look how we've treated him. How else is he to think of us?"

"Bah."

"He's right," said the toothless man. "The boy has a right to speak freely. It could have easily been him in Nikos' place."

"Nikos?"

"The boy—like you," emphasized the toothless man, "who was nailed to the wood with Jesus and Azriel. He was not much older than you."

It stopped raining.

The boy nodded. "Nikos. I saw him. Yes."

The toothless one peered at the scar-faced brute. "If he's old enough to be crucified, he's old enough to speak his mind—especially tonight."

The scar-faced man grumbled, but finally agreed. He frowned at him. "Be on your way, boy."

"Why are you looking for Judas? What will you do when you find him?"

"That's our business," said the scar-faced brute.

"He's a traitor, boy," said the toothless man.

"To whom?"

"You don't know?"

"What?"

The toothless man glanced at the lamp holder. "Tell him."

A roll of thunder could be heard in the distance.

"He's an informer."

"Tell him everything," the toothless man insisted.

"Jesus. He betrayed Jesus," the lamp holder declared. "With a kiss, my boy."

"Our . . . our Master?"

"Your master, boy," said the scar-faced man. "Not ours."

"But, why? Why?"

"That's what we want to find out."

"Then . . . then you'll kill him."

"No, my boy," the toothless man countered. "Not us. Our brigand chief Ganto wants the honor of doing that."

The boy shook his head. "Betrayed Rabbi Jesus. But why?"

"Politics. Money. Madness. It doesn't matter, boy. He's doomed," said the toothless man.

"We're all doomed," said the lamp holder, as he nudged the boy. "Do you know where you're going, boy?"

"Toward . . . toward Gethsemane."

"Why?"

"Because . . . because of Judas. What you said. If Jesus was at the garden, then my father had to be there with him. And if you say Rabbi Jesus was betrayed—"

"Yes, yes, he was betrayed and arrested at Gethsemane. That's a fact." The lamp holder checked the level of the oil that fed the struggling frame. "It's a waste of time going there, boy. That would be the last place to look for your father."

"I don't know where else to start." He bit his lower lip. "Funny."

"What?"

"Gethsemane. On Mount Olivet. It's where I was going in the first place. I guess . . . I guess now I know why."

"Leave him alone," said the toothless man.

"I'm only trying to help the boy. Look at him. What does he know?"

"As I see it, as much as any one of us, right now."

The scar-faced brute guffawed.

"Good luck to you, boy," said the toothless one.

The men left him standing in the wind and in the darkness and in the vastness of a deeper sorrow caused by the knowledge of Judas' betrayal of his Master.

God

The smaller trees and bushes and undergrowth, which had struggled against a rocky soil of poor quality and had suffered from years of inadequate rainfall, were now inundated with storm water because of poor drainage and because the water that flowed into the Garden of Gethsemane's basin washed down the hillside from Jerusalem's direction. The small grove of mature olive trees towered over the surrounding pools of murky water and lorded over the drowning shrubbery.

The boy crouched inside the dark outer rim of the olive grove beside a large tree with a wide trunk. The concealment within the gloom provided him with a sense of safety.

He studied the interior of the garden grove. He did not want to encounter another group of dangerous men. He had been lucky with the last three.

They could have been murdering scavengers capable of doing anything to seize whatever there was of value. Among that kind, even the joy of torturing the innocent was of value.

He knelt beside the large olive tree, leaned toward it, and managed to nestle the right side of his upright body within a relatively wide crevice of the gnarled tree trunk. If the crevice had been a little wider, he would have been able to conceal himself completely inside of it. The expansive branches of the tall tree were bent down over him like an inverted nest because its limbs were thick with leaves heavily saturated with water.

He shivered from exposure. Both legs were submerged in thin mud up to his thighs.

He struggled for comfort against the threatening weather: the misery of constant wetness, the frightening flash of lightning, the violent shifts of the ground, the intensity of the thunder, and the irregular nature of the wind's direction and forcefulness.

He wriggled the side of his body out of the crevice and embraced the tree; the wet bark felt slimy. He wedged his face into the crevice of the gnarled tree trunk in an attempt to hide from reality. He wept into the relative calmness of this dark and safe womb.

He did not want to find his father. He did not want to learn the truth. He wanted to remain here forever. He did not want to relinquish his memory of Rabbi Jesus' crucifixion to anyone—especially to his father, who would dismiss him, then ridicule him after his taking possession of the facts laid bare with their telling. As long as he kept silent, Jesus' final hour was his. His! He did not want to find his father who often scolded him in Rabbi Jesus' presence; he did not want to confront his father whose heart did not soften after Rabbi Jesus derided his father's senior brethren disciples when they were caught arguing over who among them was the greatest.

He had been there. And to his horror, and joy, it was he that Rabbi Jesus took hold of and put his arms around. To his horror, he could see his father's jealousy and bewilderment, as well as feel the uneasiness of the other men. To his joy, he was immersed in Jesus' affection and transformed by his word—a word so astounding that it had to be true:

"Whoever receives one child such as this in my name, receives me; and whoever receives me, receives not me but the one who sent me."

If Rabbi Jesus had not placed his arms around him in their midst, he probably would have been terrified by those words. But within Jesus' arms he realized the presence of God! God! And at that moment he was not afraid of his father's anger or jealousy. He was not afraid then as he was now.

He pushed himself away from the tree and looked into the dark reality of his surroundings.

God. Where was the presence of God?

He was no longer the same. But he did not know what he had become. And even though he was not the same, he still feared his father.

CHAPTER 5

Lepers

The boy heard masculine voices with the approach of dawn. He stood up feeling weary. He shivered as he peered unsteadily from behind the tree that had supported his back.

Because of the break in the weather and the break of day, he was able to see two silhouettes stirring about from what seemed to be their slumber. He was surprised by their proximity. One of them coughed.

The boy crouched in response then remained still until he felt certain he had not been seen. He noticed that there were two others still asleep. He exhaled slowly.

The other man spoke.

He strained to understand what the man was saying, but he was unsuccessful.

The one who coughed responded; his voice was hoarse and sick.

He struggled to see who these men were, as well as understand what they were doing. There was something dangerous about their behavior, their gestures—something. They were very nervous.

He was afraid to get closer to them; he chose to let the approaching light of the morning do that for him instead.

The man who spoke stood up and stretched. He approached the one who coughed and briefly placed the back of his right hand against the man's forehead. After a short and serious verbal exchange between them, the man who was standing approached the other two men. He nudged one with his foot and shook the other with his hand. The first man bolted upright and grumbled, the other man rolled onto his side and waved his hand. There were several verbal exchanges among them. The morning's glow increased.

The man who seemed sick released a long and ragged cough, which irritated the newly awakened pair. One of them grumbled as they rose to investigate the sick man's condition.

All four men looked mean and filthy, torn and soggy, cold and hungry and exhausted with fear and illness. Their mud-stained tunics were in tatters and clung heavily to their skins. Their feet were laden with mud as thick as clay. Their facial expressions were pinched, their eyes were hollow, their limbs gray and incomplete from the progress of their disease. Leprosy.

He slipped in the mud and splashed onto his rump.

Alarmed, the man who had grumbled turned toward his direction. "Who's there?"

He stood up and tried to hide behind the tree.

"There he is!" one of them shouted.

"It's a boy!" another declared.

"Easy prey," said the grumbler. "Get him!"

He turned away from them and ran.

They intended to harm him, unlike the others. They were a bad lot of scavenger lepers who had nothing to lose. They were going to kill him for no reason, and for nothing.

He was so scared he wanted to squeal, but he did not have the strength or the breath. He ran toward an outer darkness that was not there. He ran.

CHAPTER 6

Jeshua

The air was thick and wet. The breathless boy sat cross-legged on the ground in the center of a damp thicket near a cedar tree and waited to see if he had successfully escaped. He sat very still; he was afraid of disturbing any of the surrounding shrubbery. The perspiration that mingled with his rain-soaked tunic called attention to the uncomfortable weight of the woolen garment.

He shifted to his right side and supported himself with his right arm planted into the saturated ground. A thorn from a nearby nettle bush pricked his forearm. He flinched.

"You're not very good at concealing yourself, boy."

The boy did not recognize the voice.

"The bad ones who were after you have given up the chase. They're gone."

The boy was perplexed; he was not afraid. "I've been around lepers before."

"Lepers are like anybody else: Some are good, some are bad."

"They were going to hurt me."

"Then they were bad. Are you going to continue hiding unsuccessfully in the brush all morning?"

The boy laughed. "I succeeded with them."

The man nodded. "You must be hungry."

The boy stood up. He cleared his throat.

"Yes." The man grinned. "I thought so."

"Well. I haven't eaten."

"Come. My wagon, tent, and mules are over there."

The boy stumbled out of the thicket and followed the generous man. He was perplexed by his trust for this stranger.

After arriving at his camp, the man invited him into his tent.

For one man, the tent was extravagantly large. It was centered by three poles, about five cubits high, with two rows of shorter poles on two sides of the tent. There was not a single repair patch on the dark-brown, goat hair tent fabric.

Rich. Very rich.

The tent was divided into two living areas separated by a curtain that hung along the three
centered poles. The back half of the tent was his
sleeping area, a rare place of privacy, and the front
half was reserved for public use and hospitality.

The three sides of the front half were raised to
take advantage of the breeze and allow for protection against any sudden change in the weather or
from the slow-growing intensity of the sun.

The man sat on a mat with his back to the dark
entrance leading into the private half of the tent.
Then he pointed to a bowl, a pitcher, and a folded
cloth on a mat that was set near the front corner of
the tent. "There's water in that pitcher to wash yourself. Please. Be my guest."

"Thank you. Thank you." The boy approached
the washing area and poured water into the bowl.

The man sat quietly as the boy washed his
hands and face.

The boy dried himself with the cloth then discarded the dirty water outside the tent. Then he
poured fresh water into the bowl. He took off his
sandals and washed his feet.

"The sandals, too," said the man.

The boy glanced at him as he picked up his sandals. "Thank you." He immersed them into the

murky washbowl and cleaned off most of what clung to them. Then he dried his feet and dabbed the sandals with the cloth before putting them back on. He pitched the water outside the tent and began to pour some fresh water to rinse out the washbowl.

"Leave it for now," said the man. He indicated the mat across from where he sat with the offhanded gesture of his left hand. "Sit. Please."

The boy set down the bowl and approached the mat that was offered to him. He sat down and crossed his legs. The unanticipated comfort forced him to relax.

The man reached inside the back half of the tent and retrieved a small wineskin and two cups. "I believe you can use a little wine this morning." He poured the wine into both cups without waiting for the boy's response. He offered the boy the wine. "Here."

The boy took the cup and drank deeply without a show of gratitude, and without waiting for a blessing. "Sorry."

"For what?" The man reached into the back of the tent once again and pulled out a half loaf of bread. He tore off a generous hunk and offered it to the boy. "What's your name?"

The disregard for prayer followed by this question seeking his identity startled the boy. He snatched the bread from the man's hand and bit deeply into its coarse grain. He chewed. He studied the stranger. "What's yours?" His mouth was still full of bread, his eyes were full of suspicion.

The man laughed. He did not answer the boy's question.

The boy did not understand why he did not reveal his name to this man and yet accepted his food and drink and hospitality. He studied the man, who did not seem offended by this breach of etiquette in his tent.

The man was well groomed; his full-length beard and shoulder-length hair were thick and wavy and dark brown. His black eyes were sharp and distant and, yet, they drew you inside of them. The man had a strange appeal; his gentle voice was disarming, his confident manner was reassuring. He appeared to be in his early thirties.

The boy felt uneasy. He swallowed. He noticed the man's fastidiousness. The boy bit into his bread. The man and his tent seemed not to have been affected by the storm. He chewed.

The man's light beige tunic, gathered at the waist by a leather belt, was clean; the garment's fabric was made of expensive linen. His dark-brown cloak was also clean and dry and woven tightly with high-grade wool. His light-brown mantle was loosely draped over his head and shoulders; its lighter wool was tightly woven and was equally as expensive as the rest of his garments. Curiously, the man's unassuming manner did not call attention to this wealth.

The boy glanced at the man's feet: fine leather sandals. Clean feet. "Hmm."

"What?" The man's probing eyes were not intimidating. "More wine?"

The boy shook his head. "No." He'd never drunk wine this early in the day. He grimaced.

"After yesterday's storm, I thought you needed some."

The boy drank from his cup. The wine began to taste better. He began to feel better. He became more distant from his surroundings.

"What's your name?"

The boy hesitated. "Addan. Son of Elam. And yours?"

"Jeshua."

"Jesus!"

"Son of Shallum. It is a common name."

Addan bit his lower lip. "True. That was true until . . . until yesterday." He inhaled deeply then exhaled thoughtfully. "At least, for me. Forevermore. Jesus will always be more than a common name."

"Ahh. I see. You are a disciple of . . . of one of the three recently crucified."

"Me? A disciple?" The notion startled Addan. "I'm only a boy."

"You have your own mind. And your own soul. Don't you?"

"I . . . I do? Yes. I suppose—" Addan grinned despite his confusion. "It did not occur to me that I was allowed to—yes. I'm a disciple. Are you?"

Jeshua laughed and unintentionally reduced the boy back to his normal state of insecurity. He tore off a small piece of bread from the half loaf and popped it into his mouth. He chewed thoughtfully.

The sun was bright and hot. The gradual disappearance of the early morning's mist corresponded to the gradual increase in the humidity. The countryside glistened from yesterday's storm. The colors of everything wet were less intense: the ground, the bark on tree trunks, the leaves, everything that was not dry like the sky—where the color blue possessed a clear morning.

Addan squirmed from his lack of confidence. "Why don't you use the Latin form?"

"Of what?"

"Your name," Addan clarified.

"Oh, like your shrewd prophet-magician, is that it?"

"He was a rabbi."

"Whatever."

"And he was no magician."

"Now that's something else. I know a thing or two about magic." Jeshua regarded Addan's frown. "And my use of the word shrewd was a compliment to your . . . your rabbi—master. Whatever." Addan's frown softened. "I believe he was a man who understood his public. A Galilean. A Nazarene who had to . . . to reinvent himself. And what better way than through the language of a name. Jesus. I also use the Latin for my public: my audience. Especially because of my higher-paying Roman audiences—and for the Greeks who've Hellenized them."

"There were never many Greeks or Romans who listened to Jesus," said Addan.

"In truth, the vast majority of us have never heard him speak. Nevertheless, those few Greeks and Romans were important to him. Believe me, he knew the value of their presence."

"Hmm."

"The Latin translation of Jesus is for the high road. The Hebrew transliteration of Jeshua is for the low road."

"What road do you call this?" Addan asked.

"Ahhh. The road leading to Jerusalem. All roads."

"Jesus' true Hebrew translation is Yeshua."

"Precisely!" Jeshua's broad smile animated his expression and brightened his eyes as if oil lamp flames were shining from behind them. "All roads, and all names! Jesus, Jeshua, Yeshua, Yehashua, the variant Joshua—even the Greek, Iesous. What does it matter?"

"Well?"

"I like the form, Jeshua, best. It fits me. I like the sound of Jeshua in my home."

"Your home?"

"Yes. Here. My home—whenever I pitch my tent; where it is—home. Therefore, this—with you here—this is private. Jeshua. See?" Jeshua allowed Addan a moment to digest what he had said. "But, Jesus. Well. Publicly, it can be heard more clearly from my stage-platform to the back of the crowd. And, like I've told you, when there are higher paying Romans and Greeks in my audience—well, there it is—Jesus is the only choice."

"There can't be that many rich Greeks and Romans in your audiences."

"You're not listening, boy. It only takes a few to truly appreciate any entertainment in this part of the world and be grateful enough to show me their appreciation. And as I've indicated, even your . . . your rabbi understood that. More importantly for me, it only takes a few with money in a crowd to feel like many. One high-paying Greek and one high-paying Roman together will often amount to more money than all the copper shekels collected from a large crowd of country Galileans or city Judeans. Believe me."

Addan nodded. "I see."

By the way, are you more comfortable with Aramaic or Hebrew?"

"Either," said Addan. "Palestine needs many languages. Especially Jerusalem. My Greek and Latin are fluent as well."

"Good. Good. I can use someone to assist me."

"I'm . . . I'm not looking for an apprenticeship."

Jeshua laughed. "I'm not going to teach you anything."

Addan tried to suppress his confusion. "Ah. Well. Good. Because my father is—"

"Never mind what your father does for a living. Besides, he probably hasn't been engaged in his trade for some time. Ever since he became a follower of the one crucified yesterday. Am I right?"

"Jesus."

"Yes, yes. He claimed to be a messiah, didn't he?"

"He said—"

"Never mind. It doesn't matter." Jeshua smirked. "Your father has been useless for quite some time."

"Well, it's true he hasn't worked for . . . for a while, yes—"

"And he left you and your mother with the task of providing while he followed this crucified rabbi all over Galilee."

"Jesus had a lot to say."

"Have you ever listened to him?"

"Of course."

"No. I mean, really listen to him. I could never make any sense of his parables and stories." Jeshua shook his head emphatically. "Good performer, though. Great magician. Believe me, I know. I've studied his moves carefully. Couldn't figure them out." He nodded. "The best I've ever seen—or heard. And believe me, I've a good eye and a clear

ear. I make my own living as a sorcerer, magician, storyteller, healer, seller of potions, herbs, elixirs—whatever."

"Jesus was not a charlatan."

"Bah. Neither am I. You cut me to the quick, boy. Charlatan is too elevated a title for me. I'm simply an imposter."

"Jesus was not an imposter, either."

Jeshua tapped his chest with his right index finger. "This Jesus is."

"Jesus was—what's the difference between the two?"

"A charlatan often believes in his illusions. An imposter never does."

"Jesus was neither!"

"Be careful, boy. It's dangerous to actually believe in magic."

"He was beyond magic!"

"You see how you said that?"

"How?"

"With too much authority. With too much surety. With too much insecurity."

"But he said he would rise again."

"He said he was the Messiah. But look at him now."

"He said he was the son of the Father." The boy pouted.

"Black magic. People don't like that kind of magic affecting their own lives. Magic is safe if it's a game and if it's fun and if it remains in the future— or the past. But dare bring it into the present, into the heart, into the crowds right here in Palestine and, well, look out. You end up with confused women and children mourning the remains of a body and wondering: What happened to the magic? Black or white." Jeshua shook his head. "Bad magic. That's what he was convicted of. That's why Pilate washed his hands. What a politician. He was imitating our priests, who are professional diviners and magicians themselves and who still interpret dreams as well as secretly cast lots to consult God."

"They don't cast lots."

"What do you think their breast plates contain and represent? Where there's smoke, there's fire."

"But—"

"Secretly, boy. If it's done—and it is—it is done secretly." Jeshua laughed. "I love their hypocrisy. It's good for business. They spout the Law against magic and divination, yet they use the same means to consult God. Yes. I love all the contradictions in

43

men. I love the extremes at which men can live with hypocrisy. Like I said, it's great for business."

The boy sought clarification. "But the occult is against the Law."

"Of course. Sort of." He smiled. "But there's always a loophole, boy. Stay away from idolatrous uses, from Canaanite references and you're all right. Stay away from the present, boy. People want to trust God. They want to feel safe about the future, they want to justify the past. Idiots."

"They're afraid."

"Idiots, nonetheless. The future is an unknown. God sees to that. It's never been any different. And the past is done. If it were of any use, Palestine would not be in the condition it is in today."

"You make use of the past."

"Ha! Good one, boy. Very good. The difference between me and others is that I don't deny my con-tradictions. That's where I get my magic." Jeshua sucked at his teeth to convey his self-satisfaction. "It's very profitable, as well. How's the wine?"

"Too good."

"Meaning."

"I'm still here."

Jeshua laughed. "You have potential."

Addan grinned. He could not stop himself from being drawn to this charismatic man with an interesting temperament and with a respectful manner that gave him confidence—unlike his father, who was always critical of him, always watching for his next mistake. He remained perpetually nervous at his father's workshop. He turned the potter's wheel either too slowly or too quickly; he placed either too little wood or too much wood into the kiln. Something. There was always something that he didn't do right and, therefore, there was always some disapproval that destroyed his confidence.

"Relax, boy. I'm not your father."

"I know."

"Neither was the crucified one."

"He spoke of the Father."

"Yes, yes. The Father, the Father. Look where that got him." Jeshua chuckled. "Abandoned by the Father, I hear."

Addan set down his cup and stood up.

"Don't be offended, Addan. That's your problem. And your father's problem. You take everything too seriously. Sit down. You're not going anywhere."

Addan sat down, picked up his cup, and drank the rest of the wine.

"More?"

Addan hesitated. "Yes."

"Good." Jeshua's eyes sparkled with approval as he poured more wine into Addan's cup. "Like I said, you'll do."

"Doing what?"

"Gathering, my boy. Gathering shekels and drachmas and denarii from my nervous flocks seeking physical and spiritual comfort and healing." He whispered. "I need you to get the money while I work the crowds. There is a lot to be made here in the next few days. There are plenty of people looking for comfort—other than from wine."

"You'd earn money from those who are suffering and vulnerable with grief?"

"Of course. That's the quickest and most profitable way to make it, and the most satisfying for all concerned. I earn what I'm worth. They buy whatever comforts them inwardly: tricks or visions, teachings or stories. Whatever."

Addan nodded. "All right. All right. How do I collect from those in the crowd?"

"How? By smiling and being charming and by whispering, 'thank you.' But don't avoid taking or stealing or lifting whatever there is of value—of course, do so without getting caught."

Addan did not blink his eyes at what Jeshua was instructing him to do. "I see. And what should I collect?"

Jeshua was amused. "What?" The expression on his face flattened. "Shekels or leptons. No coin is too small."

"What if I find a mina?"

Jeshua howled. "You might as well have said, what if I find a talent?" He laughed again. "Not in the crowd that you and I will be working. Never. You'd be lucky to find a day's pay in most purses. A mina would take a full season to earn, and a talent, well, a talent would take a full year! Ha. You'll not find anybody like that listening to me." He waved his left hand dismissively at the boy. "Expect leptons and shekels, drachmas and staters, quadrans and denarii. Forget talents or minas or . . . or gold aurei—anything gold will be guarded by their life and, therefore, discovered lost or stolen immediately. That person would be after blood. We don't want a blood incident. Understand?"

Addan shrugged his shoulders. "I . . . I think so."

"You'd better. This is not a game. Blood or no blood, this is still an act of life and death to most people in my audience."

"Then . . . then why do it?"

"Because. It's there. Because. It's dangerous. Because. You'll never have lived so intensely in all your life, boy. You'll see."

"You are an opportunist."

"I'm also a cynic. Read the Greeks, boy. Can you read Greek?"

"No."

"Doesn't matter. You've a good memory."

"You don't know me," Addan countered.

"Your intelligence indicates that."

Addan liked the compliment. With increased confidence, he extended his already empty cup to indicate that he wanted more wine.

"Already? You couldn't be that familiar with wine. Especially in this hour of the day."

"I don't care."

"Good for you."

Jeshua pulled the stopper from the wineskin and poured Addan another full cup of wine. "There. Drink up. Drink as much as you want today. You can sleep it off."

Addan drank. He was already drunk. "Sleep what off?"

"You'll see."

"I'm seeing pretty good right now."

"Yes." Jeshua grinned. "You'll see. Besides, there's no use breaking camp on a Sabbath to seek one of Jerusalem's marketplaces in order to set up the wagon ahead of time. That wouldn't look good to our prospective audience."

"Yes," said Addan, as if he understood what Jeshua meant by our or what he meant when he expressed concern over the Sabbath.

"So, drink up. Enjoy. Tonight you and I will sleep well so we can be alert and on our game tomorrow."

"Tomorrow?" Addan slurred. "What game?"

"I told you. I need an assistant. People want comfort and reassurance after a public execution. They want entertainment. Healing. Some indication that they aren't next. That they are safe." Jeshua chuckled. "Sheep. Poor, poor sheep. To them, it's real. To us, it's a game." He drank deeply from his cup. "We're all doomed, boy."

"Jesus would have disagreed with you."

"Don't you have eyes, boy? The crucified one has just demonstrated that the darkness awaits us all. In the end, we are all abandoned. In the end, suffering prevails. In the end, nothing is left." Jeshua squinted at Addan with powerfully dark eyes. "There's no hope. No meaning. Nothing matters."

Addan placed his empty cup on the mat and crossed his arms over his chest. He swayed from side to side; his speech was slurred. "You . . . you frighten me."

"Me? After seeing what happened to your rabbi, mere words frighten you? Hmm. I'm beginning to have my doubts about you."

"At least I'm . . . I'm not completely pre-dictable."

"Ha!" The boy's remark surprised Jeshua. "Very good, young man." He reached inside his tent. "Very good." He presented a bowl of figs, then took one for himself, before placing the bowl on the mat between them. "These are good." He bit into the fresh fig and enjoyed the sweetness. "Eat."

Addan took one of the figs and carefully nib-bled off one end. "Sweet. Good."

"You'll eat well today, as well."

"That's not what I'm worried about."

"What are you worried about?"

"About what I'll be doing tomorrow. With you. Instead of finding my father. Instead of obeying my mother. Instead of mourning Jesus' death."

"Then it's settled. A few days in the life with another Jesus." He grinned. "A darker side, let's say."

"I don't know why that doesn't matter to me."

"Yes. I know. That's the thrill of temptation. Believe me, boy, I know." Jeshua bit into another fig and watched the boy bite into the one he had started after finishing his third cup of wine. He poured the boy another drink.

CHAPTER 7

Addan

Addan tossed and turned miserably in one of Jeshua's spare pallets throughout the night. Despite the chill in the air, Addan felt hot—then cold, then hot again. He fought with the dry blanket that covered him.

He awoke several times during the dark hours feeling thirsty, but he could not rise from his pallet to get a drink of water. His head felt heavy. His eyes felt as if they were stuffed with wool. His hair was matted against his head with perspiration. He felt sick.

Dreams assaulted him and drove him into a half-consciousness that was neither wakefulness nor slumber; each time he tried to remember what brought him to the surface, the dream simply faded and then disappeared. He could not hold onto it. He could not think:

My God, my God. Help me, my God.

A new kind of storm engulfed Addan, which swept away his past and intensified his anger toward his father's authority and illuminated his resentment toward his mother's possessiveness; his father was brutal, his mother was relentless: Both were suffocating him, killing him—or so it felt.

Addan sat up in a fit and managed to wipe the sweat from his forehead. His head was pounding. He wanted to die. "Father. Jesus. Mother."

He plopped onto his back—hot and thirsty, exhausted and sick. He turned onto his right side and vomited. Then a dark darkness carried him into more bad dreams.

CHAPTER 8

Magic

Jeshua laughed. "At least you had sense enough not to get sick on a mat."

Addan opened his eyes; Jeshua was standing beside him. "Thirsty."

"Yes, yes," said Jeshua. "Get up."

"Sick."

"I know, I know." Jeshua offered Addan a full cup of wine. "Here. Drink this."

Addan managed to sit up after tremendous effort. He reached for the cup. "Water."

"Wine."

Addan pulled his hand back as if he'd touched something very hot. "Never again."

"Drink it. It'll do your head good. Trust me."

"My head feels as if there's someone inside hitting me with a hammer."

Jeshua laughed.

"I'm glad I amuse you."

"Take the cup and drink it. I promise you'll feel better."

Reluctantly, Addan accepted the cup. He studied it.

"Drink it."

Addan brought the wine to his mouth, but its odor gagged him. He pulled the cup away. He swallowed hard to keep himself from getting sick. Then he looked at Jeshua's stern countenance. "All right. All right." He brought the cup to his mouth and drank. It was as if he were putting out an internal fire. He took another drink.

Jeshua chuckled. "Good. Drink it all." He approached the entrance that led him into the front half of the tent. "I'll be right back. Have it finished by the time I return." He left Addan alone to deal with his misery.

Addan took a deep breath, exhaled slowly, then drank what was left in his cup. He set the cup beside his wrecked pallet and felt a kind of glow invade his body and soften his head pain. He was going to live. "Thank you, Lord."

Addan pushed his blanket aside and stood up. He felt weak. He adjusted his loincloth. He scanned the tent's interior.

His tunic was draped over the baskets, his sandals were set nearby, and his woolen cap had been placed on top of the sandals. He wobbled as he stepped toward his clothes.

He shook out his damp tunic before he put it on. Then he put on his woolen cap and his sandals.

Jeshua appeared at the entrance with a small wooden bucket. "How are you doing?"

Addan took a single unsteady step toward him. "I think I'm all right."

"Good." Jeshua set the bucket by the interior entranceway. "Come on."

Addan followed him through the entranceway, across the open hospitality side of the tent, then outside.

Jeshua took several steps away from his tent and peered into the distance at Jerusalem. He waited for Addan to come alongside him. "Help me take down this tent and pack it into the wagon. We need to get to the marketplace nearest Golgotha."

"That would be at Damascus Gate," said Addan.

"Splendid. You'll show me the way."

The tent was stretched out over nine poles that were held in place by ropes that were tied to leather loops sewn onto the tent.

Addan started to loosen one of the taut ropes near the wooden tent peg that had been driven into the ground.

There were nine ropes in all: two for each corner post plus one for each of the two outside center posts, which provided the tent its stability.

"Hold it there, boy. Help me load my wagon first."

Addan followed Jeshua back into the open, front half of the tent, then inside the private half. He scanned the interior as if it had been the first time he'd seen it.

There was a basket filled with food and another basket filled with a small iron cooking pot, a couple of wooden utensils, and several clay bowls and platters. There was a wineskin hanging from one of the center posts, a thick and comfortable-looking sleeping pallet on the ground to one side and a disheveled sleeping pallet on the other side, a pair of woolen floor mats between the pallets, and an unlit oil lamp.

Jeshua knelt at the foot of his pallet and began rolling up his bed. "Stage those baskets behind my wagon."

Addan felt embarrassed about his sweat-stained pallet and the congealed vomit beside it. "I'll take care of—"

"Don't worry about the pallets. I'll take care of both of them." Jeshua acknowledged what Addan was referring to. He reached for the bucket that he had brought in with him on the way back inside, positioned the bucket above the vomit, and poured its sandy contents over it. He peered at Addan. "We've all done that. All of us."

"We—we're . . . we're not supposed to."

"Bah. Grow up. Stage the baskets. Go on. The work will do you good."

Addan picked up the food basket, carried it outside the tent, and approached the canopy-enclosed wagon with four wheels, each constructed with eight spokes. The wagon's canopy was extravagantly made of three panels—a front, middle, and rear—with the same dark-brown woven goat hair as Jeshua's tent. Each panel was roughly stitched onto the four ribs of wood that supported the wagon's canopy.

There were two hobbled mules grazing nearby. The wagon's harness arrangement was built to use them both to pull the wagon. The mules resembled horses, but they were shorter. Their thick heads had short manes and long ears. Their short legs ended with small feet and their short tails ended with tufts of long hair.

Addan's headache had lessened but he still felt queasy. He rubbed his knotted stomach.

Jeshua approached Addan from behind carrying the rolled-up bed pallets and floor mats. "Are you going to stand there all morning or are you going to help me break camp?"

"You travel in great luxury," said Addan.

"A man must appear profitable in order to remain profitable."

"What do you sell?"

"I've already told you, my boy. But that still is a good question, considering the effects and aftereffects of the wine. A very good question."

Jeshua set the rolled bed pallets and floor mats on the ground. He unlatched a short rope from a wooden peg on each side of the wagon and lowered the rear gate-platform. He reached into the wagon's bed and, one at a time, pulled out three support posts that he let fall to the ground. Then he raised the rear gate-platform until it was even with the wagon's bed.

Jeshua positioned each support post underneath the rear gate and slipped each of the post's top ends into the deep and corresponding circular notches that were cut into the underside edge of the rear gate that was now transformed into a platform. He carefully positioned the posts so that they stood straight on the ground and supported the end of the platform that extended about four cubits beyond the rear of the wagon. After he positioned all three support posts and aligned the side holes in each post with the holes bored through the front edge of the platform into the circular notches, he reached into a small wicker basket that sat near the right rear corner of the wagon's gate and pulled out three wooden tee-pegs and a wooden mallet. He inserted the tee-pegs into each hole and tapped them into place with the wooden mallet to secure the support poles into place. "There you are."

"What is that?"

"It's . . . it's theatre. A stage."

Addan studied the platform. "I—see." His lower lip crept over the top of his upper lip.

"You'll see." Jeshua pulled out a wooden box from within the wagon and used it as a step to climb onto the platform. He was an imposing figure standing on the stage-platform. He stamped his right foot to check the stage floor's stability. "Dreams, my boy. I'm a seller of dreams. Miracles, my boy. I'm a seller of magic." He untied a rope on the rear top of both sides of the wagon and allowed a square piece of tent fabric to unfurl and curtain off the interior of the wagon. "I am also a seller of tonics and healing potions." He knelt on his right knee and waved his hands ritually until a small clay vial with a wooden stopper wrapped in a piece of fabric appeared in his right hand from what seemed to have been mid air. "Water and honey and a bit of rind of the pomegranate for a dash of yellow coloring." Jeshua tapped the vial with the forefinger of his left hand. "These containers are what cost me. And that will be one of your duties."

"Doing—what?"

"Well. After the sales are made, I want you to gather the discarded vials—if there are any. Don't worry. Nobody will notice, or care, since you'll have been mingling with the crowd all along. About half my costumers drink and discard them immediately."

He admired the vial. "Yes, honey and water and my incantations can earn quite a profit."

Jeshua waved his left hand over the vial in his right. The vial disappeared.

Addan was impressed.

Jeshua stood up, turned toward the curtain, and reached behind it. He pulled out a placard and hung it from the top rear rib—one of four ribs—that held the wagon's fabric cover in place. A single phrase was boldly written in four languages from the top to the bottom of the placard: Greek, Latin, Hebrew, Aramaic—the first two were read from left to right and the second two were read from right to left.

Addan squinted at the Aramaic and the Hebrew lines and read haltingly. "Healing . . . Tonics . . . for Sale."

"I thought you said you couldn't read."

"Greek. But I can read some Aramaic and Hebrew—and a few words of Latin. Why the placard?"

"Why not?"

Addan pursed his lips. "Well. Most of the people who come to the market to sell in Jerusalem can't read. In fact, most of the city's house servants and poor city dwellers who come to the market to buy can't read either."

"Ahh. Very good. But the placard is aimed at those rich city dwellers, who come to the market instead of sending their servants or slaves. They're the ones with real currency."

"Even the lowest bronze lepton is real currency."

"True. But the poor city dweller carrying bronze almost never has silver to exchange." Jeshua shook his head for emphasis. "No. Bronze rarely leads to silver. In fact, many of those in the bronze class are so poor that they can only offer me payment with a loaf of bread or a small basket of fruit or something else of value."

"I . . . I don't understand. I thought you said—"

"Never mind what I said. Barter, boy. The illiterate, the poor, and the common generally try to barter the excess goods they have to spare."

"Bread is good payment."

"Sure. But I can only eat so many loaves. And, in truth, bartering oftentimes hinders me from keeping my eye out for the few richer ones in my audience who can read and, therefore, possibly lead to silver shekels or denarii or more."

"But—"

"If you can live with your crucified rabbi's contradictions, you can live with mine."

Addan did not know how to argue this point. Jeshua's comparison to Rabbi Jesus startled him into confusion, into no thought at all. He trembled. He finally countered by changing the subject. "Why mules?"

Jeshua was amused. "They're hardier and more surefooted than donkeys. They're less prone to disease than an ass or a horse."

"Really?"

"And, as you should know, they're highly valued as load bearers and they are especially prized because of their patience at pulling a wagon. Besides, they are also stronger and more courageous than horses."

"But they are hybrids."

Jeshua feigned innocence. "I did not breed them. I purchased them, my boy." He chuckled. "I love the hypocrisy of our people."

"I . . . I don't understand what you mean."

"The Law, my boy. Like I've told you, our people condemn the use and profit of magic and divination, yet we often secretly use the same means to consult God. It is also contrary to the Law to breed animals from mixed parentage, yet we can purchase and employ these hybrids—as long as we don't breed them, of course." He chuckled. "Loopholes, boy. We know how to thread a very small needle."

"What needle?"

"Never mind." Jeshua jumped off the stage-platform. "You're supposed to be helping me break camp and load this wagon." Jeshua picked up the rolled pallets and mats. "Follow me." He stepped onto the wooden box, then onto the stage. "With the basket, boy. With the basket." He brushed aside the backstage curtain leading into the wagon and stepped inside. Addan climbed onto the platform and followed him into the wagon. Jeshua laid the rolls on the floor on the left side of the wagon bed. "Place the baskets over there, hang the wineskin and waterskin on those hooks, and put the oil lamp inside that box."

"Right." Addan felt the curtain against his back as he paused just inside the wagon's rear threshold. He sensed magic within the shade of this wagon's interior. Somehow, everything seemed to sparkle with meaning and life and . . . and the surrounding objects did not seem inanimate.

Along the entire length, on both sides of the wagon's interior, there were two shelves with countless miniature clay vials that were kept in place by wood facings, four fingers wide, that ran the entire lower half of each shelf to prevent the tightly packed vials from dancing off the shelves while the wagon traveled across the rugged countryside.

The front end of the wagon was curtained off in the same manner as the rear of the wagon, except that there was a slight angle in the drop of the curtain, which outlined the back of the driver's bench. Two large, side-by-side chests sat behind the bench with enough clearance to allow the thickly woven curtain to drop between the chests and the rear of the driver's bench, as well as to allow the trunks to be opened without obstruction. The trunks were painted with red and blue and yellow swirls that randomly intersected each other.

When he started to take the food basket to the right side of the wagon, Addan bumped his head against a strange object, which floated from the ceiling of the canopy. He halted abruptly and glanced at the dancing, tree-like object above him, then realized that there were others like it and, yet, none of the dangling objects were the same.

Closer study revealed that these floating objects were crystals of varying sizes that hung from the tree-like objects. Each crystal was wrapped with pieces of fishing net. One end of a leather cord was tied to the net and the other end of the cord was tied to a stick.

Addan set down the basket of food. He pursed his lips.

The crystals that hung from the ends of the sticks seemed off-centered and impossible and, yet, they were overhead: floating lazily from the ribs that held the wagon's canopy in place. He studied the one he bumped into—it was the least complex of the mobile sculptures.

A leather cord was tied to the top of the third rib and attached to the middle of a length of stick. The end of a leather cord was tied to one end of the same stick, and the other end of the cord was tied to a netted crystal. Another leather cord was attached to the opposite end of the stick. However, the other end of the cord was tied to the center of a second length of stick, which had two small netted crystals attached to cords that were tied to both ends of that stick. Because of the movement of the wagon and, in the case of the above floating mobile that his head bumped into, both sticks in the mobile struggled to float horizontally as they danced and bobbed and twirled with the three attached crystals in a haphazard orbit limited by the length of the cords and the sticks.

Addan was fascinated by the magical pinpoints of light that these mobile crystal sculptures created against the inside of the canopy. The crystals caught the light from the partial opening of the rear curtain then released the captured light as twinkling specks that danced overhead like stars in the sky. "Stars in the sky."

Jeshua winked at Addan. "You're going to be all right." He emphasized his approval with a nod. "You're going to do fine today."

Addan tapped the smallest of the three crystals that, when he squinted his eyes, appeared to hang from a bobbing branch of an upside-down sky. "Why?"

"Because you have imagination, boy. And, you're neither afraid nor resentful of me no matter what I say to you or how I say it."

Addan grinned. "Should I be?"

"Come on. Let's finish loading this wagon."

Once loaded, they loosened the tent ropes that were tied to the ground pegs and collapsed the tent. They gathered the tent poles and loaded them into the wagon. Then they coiled the tent ropes and tied the coils to the leather pendants that were permanently sewn onto the tent's exterior before they smoothed and flattened the tent on the ground and folded it into one large rectangle. They loaded the tent into the wagon then deconstructed the stage-platform. Once the rear of the wagon was latched up and secured, they unhobbled and harnessed the mules. Both animals were gentle and cooperative, even content at having been harnessed to pull the wagon.

Jeshua climbed into the front of the wagon and sat on the left side of the driver's bench. He untied the reins from the wagon's hitching post and separated the right from the left in preparation to drive the wagon. He noticed Addan standing beside the wagon with both arms akimbo. "What are you admiring now?"

"That's quite a rig you have there for one man."

"It's not as much as you think, boy." He leaned toward Addan. "Imagine. This is everything I own in the world. It's my home. It's my business. It's all that stands between me: The Master of Secrets, and me: the beggar man. Are you going to stand there all day or are you going to climb into this wagon with me?"

Addan climbed onto the right side of the wagon and sat on the driver's bench next to Jeshua. "The Master of Secrets?"

"I haven't shown you that placard yet. The one I showed you was for the physical healing part of my . . . my performance. While I'm selling my 'healing tonics,' I'll need you to operate within the crowd. This will establish you among them. Then, down comes 'The Master of Secrets' placard, and I transform myself into a magician and hopefully transform them into forgetting themselves while you—"

Addan's eyes widened—"yes, you reach into their purses for whatever you can get."

"You mean, steal."

"Shush. Never use that word."

"But that's what it is."

"Ownership is an illusion. Like everything else. It's the root of all evil. Your—" Jeshua cleared his throat. "God has made that very clear. Ask the Pharisees yourself. Your own rabbi would have agreed."

"Yes. But this . . . this so-called illusion has consequences."

"Only if you're caught." Jeshua leaned toward the boy. "Just don't get caught." He sat up straight. "Besides, think of whatever you're able to . . . to procure as . . . as payment. Yes. Payment for the entertaining services that I'll be providing—payment that usually goes unpaid. In a manner of speaking, you're keeping them honest by making sure they've paid for my valuable services. See?"

"I'm . . . I'm not sure I'm going to be able to do this . . . this, this procuring that's not stealing for unrequested services rendered."

Jeshua chortled deeply from his belly. "You're sharp, my boy. Quick. Perceptive. Even articulate."

"What?"

"You have a gift for gab."

Addan shook his head. "Still. I'm not sure—"

Jeshua nudged Addan's left shoulder affection-ately with his lowered right shoulder. "Of course you can. You'll see. Once you're among them and infected with the energy and the excitement of my show along with the energy and excitement of my audience—well, you'll see. You can do anything."

"I'll be too nervous."

"Nonsense."

"I'll . . . I'll be caught tugging at their purses."

"Listen to me, boy. Trust me. My magic will have them so fascinated that they won't feel anything you do to them, once I cast my spell on them."

"Like the one you have on me?"

Jeshua's expression broadened with a genuine grin. "Ho, ho. See? I can't deceive you with flattery. You're your own man. So trust me, boy. Trust me."

Addan squirmed in his seat. "All right. All right. I'll . . . I'll try."

Jeshua nodded with approval. "Good. Do the best you can. That'll be fine." He reached inside the wagon, retrieved what appeared to be a small wine-skin, and tossed it onto Addan's lap. "Here. Drink."

"I can't drink anymore this morning."

"Where's Damascus Gate?"

"I can't—"

"It's water, my boy. Water. Where?"

Addan pointed easterly. "That way." He pulled the stopper from the waterskin, brought the opened neck to his mouth, and drank greedily.

Jeshua flicked the reins and whistled at his mules. "Yeaa! Let's go, Haga." He whistled again. "Beba. Let's go. Yeaa! Take us to Jerusalem."

The wagon pitched downward and caused Addan to spill water all over himself. He almost dropped the waterskin when he grabbed a hold of the forward rib nearest him to prevent himself from being tossed out of the wagon.

"Hang on, boy. You are about to live like you have never lived before." Jeshua flicked the reins again and forced the mules to increase their speed. The wagon jostled and bumped and pitched from side to side from the rocks and the ruts in the terrain. "Don't worry, boy. This adventure will get smoother once we reach the Roman road."

"I . . . I hope so."

Jeshua smirked. "It's Jerusalem, boy. There's nothing to worry about. Only rabbi-prophets and political rebels are executed there. Rome has nothing to fear from us."

"I'm not afraid of Rome. But I am afraid of Roman legionnaires and the couriers who use those roads. Not to mention those legionnaires who work to keep the roads in good repair. Their nasty dispositions make them dangerous."

"Ha! Good one. That means you know how to be careful."

Addan hesitated. "Right."

Jeshua winked. "Whatever that means, boy. Whatever that means."

Wagon travel eased considerably as soon as they reached the stone of the Roman road that led to Damascus Gate as well as to Golgotha.

Addan sat up more attentively as he peered into the distance. "My God. Golgotha. We are going to travel past Golgotha."

"You're the one leading the way."

"I know, I know, but. . . ."

"What. What?"

"I forgot we had to ride by Golgotha and . . . and—"

"You want to go another way?"

"No. No." Addan did not feel sick anymore.

CHAPTER 9

Truth

Jeshua brought the mules to a halt when they reached the closest point to Golgotha from the road. He noted Addan's distress. "Easy, boy. Are you all right?"

"I don't know. No."

"Get in line with the rest of us."

Addan peered over his right shoulder: Golgotha appeared abandoned aside from two Roman guards.

Two of the three crosses on the barren hill were occupied, but the one between them had been stripped of its victim, Jesus.

"He's gone!" Addan stood up on the wagon's foot rest. "He's gone." He scanned the place of the skull.

"Well. That surely is different. I've never heard of anybody being brought down from the wood. "Ever."

Addan's eyes were wide with confusion and concern. "He must be dead. Don't you think? Dead."

"And buried and forgotten by all except for . . . for his invisible sister disciples and their children—"

"And . . ." Addan sat down on the wagon's bench feeling defeated. "And his frightened brother disciples who are probably, well—who must be in hiding."

"Yes. Your father would be among them."

"Yes. My . . . my father would be . . . be among them."

Jeshua touched Addan gently on the shoulder with his right hand. "Easy, there. Do you need another cup of wine to steady yourself?"

Addan shook his head. "Wine cannot ease my sorrow, my . . . my sense of loss."

"Good. It's better to face things as they are."

"Reality from a magician?"

"Hmm. You are sharp, young man. You can become my apprentice if you want to."

"I do have a father, who has a trade."

"Good. Good. A loyal son, as well."

"And a mother."

Jeshua chuckled. "You're too loyal, and too honest, my boy. Forget that nonsense. I believe your rabbi has done you a disservice in this harsh world of ours."

"That's right. Father can think whatever he wants about me. And Mother, too."

"Good one, boy." Jeshua tried unsuccessfully to uncover any facetiousness in the tone of Addan's remark. He was caught off guard with surprise. "As I see it, you're too young and tender to know anything about this . . . this so-called love and goodness that he has been purported to have taught."

"Pur—what?"

"Professed to be, my boy. And often falsely."

"He spoke of truth, of loving one another, of honesty. I heard this myself. And I'm old enough to know—"

"What would you know about the nonsense of truth? And love? Ha! It's the other side of hate."

"I didn't say I understood him." Addan grimaced. "And I don't understand you, either. What do you mean?"

"Darkness and light. Evil and good. You can't have one without the other."

"And?"

"You can't love or be loved unless you've hated or have been hated. And as for honesty, you can't be

77

honest unless you've been dishonest—that is, in order to know what it is. You would have had to lie and cheat and steal in order to know what it was to be good—really good."

"That's not what—"

"Never mind what your Jesus said. He's dead, remember?"

"He was good. Really good. Not like me or you. He never lied or cheated or stole."

"Then he wasn't human. And if he wasn't human, what good was he as an example to us? To all the nobodies in the world? To this pathetic and sick human race?"

"Yes," Addan whispered, almost to himself. "Like you and me."

"What good would that be?"

Addan stared at the place of the skull and tried to remember what Jesus was like on the day he was executed.

Addan leaned his head against the canopy rib. He felt empty and barren. He felt impotent and helpless when Rabbi Jesus fell to the ground where the legionnaire struck Jesus twice with a leather whip. The legionnaire was ordered to stop by the centurion in charge who then ordered a man in the crowd to take the burden of Rabbi Jesus' cross.

The frightened man declared himself an innocent Cyrene minding his own business. As he pleaded with the centurion to assign someone else to the task, Rabbi Jesus managed to push his chest off the ground with his shaking arms and sit back on his knees in order to address the crowd of women and children who were bewailing and lamenting him.

Addan could have sworn that Rabbi Jesus was speaking directly to him. But his sister swore that Jesus had spoken directly to her.

She was right, of course—that is, Jesus was speaking to the Daughters of Jerusalem with whom Addan was standing: his mother, his sister, his aunt, his friends, and other sister disciples and their children. Jesus' voice was weak, but steady:

"*Daughters of Jerusalem do not weep for me, but for yourselves and for your children. For behold, days are coming in which men will say, 'Blessed are the barren, and the wombs that never bore, and breasts that never nursed.' Then they will begin to say to the mountains, 'Fall upon us,' and to the hills, 'Cover us!' For if in the case of green wood they do these things, what is to happen in the case of the dry wood?*"

The feminine sea of brown and beige tunics and mantles conveyed plain modesty and virtue, despite their poverty. All hair was covered. Most faces were veiled. Every feminine feature, every woman's figure was hidden beneath loose-fitting garments.

They mourned. They wept. They bowed subserviently. Yet, these women managed to maintain their soundness of mind.

Why is Jesus warning his mother and my mother and—?

Addan turned away from Jesus in order to see what he was seeing and—

All mothers. Jesus is speaking to all mothers and warning them about a coming persecution. But . . . but the persecution is already here. Isn't it? Isn't it?

The women could not stop crying. Even Jesus' calm eyes were not enough. Addan turned back to Rabbi Jesus.

What does Jesus see? Why does he feel sorry for us and not for himself? His eyes. There is destruction in them. He sees destruction in the future—the future. Our destruction. Women and children. He knows that women and children are going to suffer the most. Die the most.

Addan rubbed his eyes, blinked hard, then squinted at Rabbi Jesus. Jesus. Their eyes met. Addan felt strange when he heard Jesus' mind:

Green wood represents Israel and me; dry wood represents Israel without me. Do you see what Rome is doing with innocent green wood? Imagine what Rome is going to do with guilty dry wood. There will be no escape from suffering then. These are words of pity, not of condemnation.

Addan trembled. He did not understand what was happening to him. He fell to his knees. Again, Addan heard his rabbi's mind:

I am suffering unto death. For them, I am. There is no other way.

The women surrounding Jesus raised a death-wail for him as Jesus raised his death-wail for Jerusalem. But the women did not need to hear him: They were mothers, all mothers who understood pain and sorrow; birth and death; here and now.

Tears streamed down Addan's eyes. Confusion muddled his thoughts.

The Roman legionnaire kicked Jesus. "Get up!"

Jesus rose to his feet and stumbled sideways toward Addan, who quickly stood up and caught him before he fell.

Skin and bones. Blood and sweat.

Addan felt his rabbi's right hand on his left shoulder. He felt Rabbi Jesus steady himself before he took his next step toward Golgotha.

The legionnaire raised his whip. "Get going!"

Addan stepped between the Roman soldier and Rabbi Jesus. "He's going."

The guard struck Addan with the whip. The centurion in charge ordered the legionnaire to stop when he raised the whip to strike Addan again.

Addan did not feel the blow. He was prepared not to feel the second blow. The women, however, felt all his pain. And all his rabbi's pain. The women understood pain. They understood the pain that his rabbi had taken on!

Before Addan could understand what he was experiencing, the legionnaire with the whip pushed him back into the huddle of women. Somehow, Addan knew this was going to happen.

Coward. Coward.

Addan remained within their relative safety, their painful invisibility.

"What good would that be?" Jeshua nudged Addan with his elbow thus turning Addan's mind away from the past of the distant crosses on Golgotha to the present with Jeshua. "What good would that be?" He noted Addan's frown. "Are you all right?"

Addan shrugged his shoulders. "I was there. My Jesus. He was there . . . there for me and . . . and I halfheartedly tried to be there for him."

"Easy, boy." Jeshua leaned toward Addan. "Halfhearted? Halfhearted? That sounds like you did something."

"No." The firmness in Addan's voice grew. "If I had, I would have succeeded. But my effort was cowardly. Halfhearted. Pathetic and sick like the human race. I knew I'd fail. I knew I'd be brushed aside as unimportant. I knew I was safe among invisible women and realized that I was invisible too. And I knew my performance was good but not honest— no, wait—not truthful."

"Don't take me so literally, boy. At least, not yet."

"Why?"

"Because you're too hard on yourself. I need to break you of that."

"Well." Addan seriously considered Jeshua's answer. "I know something about the truth. I did learn something from Rabbi Jesus."

"What?"

"How to recognize the truth even though I never learned how to act truthfully."

"Good God. Like I said, this Jesus has done you a disservice, boy."

"I'm not a boy!"

"Hmm. Alright."

"And in truth, I've learned nothing from him." He chuckled. "In truth. See what I mean? I've learned nothing."

"That's hard for me to believe."

"I'm with you, aren't I? I contradict myself, don't I? And I'm ready, even eager, to steal into this—this darkness and light, into this evil and good you speak about." Addan grimaced. "But . . . but why?"

Jeshua whistled at the mules and flicked their reins. "If I knew the answer to that I wouldn't be who I am either. But I am. And so are you." He whistled. "Let's go, Haga!" He flicked the reins harder. "You, too, Beba. Take Jeshua and Addan into Jerusalem. City of Peace. Of kings. Of gold. Of God." He whistled again. The wagon pitched downward as he cursed lovingly at the mules. He laughed. "Take us to Jerusalem before we continue to think."

CHAPTER 10

Azriel

Jeshua suddenly steered the wagon toward Golgotha.

"What are doing? Where are you going?"

"Curiosity has got the best of me. Sorry. You're not to blame."

Terror washed across Addan's face. "You'll not find anything on Golgotha now. Can't you see?"

"Let me be the judge of that."

"But he's no longer there." Addan was in a near panic. "My rabbi has been taken down from the wood. He's gone! Can't you see?"

"Calm yourself. There's nothing to be afraid of."

Addan gripped the front edge of the driver's bench with both hands, which were also pressed against the side of his thighs.

Jeshua laughed. "I can't go into Jerusalem with-out having seen this place for myself. My magic, my

85

sorcery, my divination has to appear authentic, has to appear otherworldly—but from there. It has to start from there." Despite the residual wetness of the surrounding landscape, Jeshua spat over his left shoulder from the habit of sitting behind mules that kicked up sand and dirt on normally dry terrain. "I need the facts. I have to be able to describe Golgotha accurately. I need the sense of it." He inhaled forcefully then exhaled as if he were clearing his lungs for a purpose. "I need to smell the death it contains." He glanced at Addan. "Spirits, boy. They're always lurking about. We can't see them, but they're there. Spirits."

"But . . . but you won't see Rabbi Jesus."

"Spirits. Maybe his spirit. Besides, there are others dead or dying on the wood. Therefore, I'll have seen Jesus." Jeshua pointed at Golgotha. "See? There are two still left up there, like you said. One of them still seems to be alive."

"Yes. The big one."

"Did you know him?"

"No. Of course not. They say he was a common bandit. A thief. They say he was even a, well. . . ."

"Well?"

"Nothing."

"You're not sure you believe what they said."

"Well."

"Therefore, you're not sure who he was?"

"I . . . I guess."

"And you're not even sure who your Rabbi Jesus was."

"Now wait there. He was never suspected of being—"

"A criminal?" Jeshua chuckled. "He was executed with them because he was as common as them—and as common as you and me." He leaned forward on the driver's bench and relaxed the reins as he pondered deeply. "Yes. Of course." His eyes sparkled suddenly. "A common bandit. A thief. That one up there who is still alive. He's my Jesus. Yes." He turned to Addan as he flicked the reins. "Do you know his name?"

Addan was shocked. "His name?"

"The big one up there who's still dying."

"Yes." Although Addan was growing accustomed to Jeshua's cryptic remarks and unpredictable behavior, he felt terribly unsettled by Jeshua's irreverent remarks concerning—

"Well? What's the name?"

"Az . . . Azriel."

"Azriel." Jeshua glanced at the cluster of crosses. "Hmm. Poor dumb creature. And the other?"

Addan searched his memory. "I think—wait. Nikos. That's it. A Greek youth."

Jeshua studied Golgotha as the mules brought them closer. "Yes, yes. A Greek. No matter. A follower." He squinted. "His eyes appear to be plucked. Hmm. He's already dead. No matter. This is good information nonetheless."

"Good information for what?"

"You'll see."

"Please, Jeshua, please—let's not go there."

"What are you afraid of? It's over. There's nothing left but one dead and one dying man. Even the guards are probably looking forward to being relieved of their duty from this God-forsaken place."

Jeshua drove the wagon to the foot of the mound. "Whoa. Right there, girls. Whoa."

Death hung in the air.

There were two auxiliary garrison guards. One was asleep and the other was crouched near a small fire that he was tending. He seemed unconcerned, even disinterested in the wagon's approach.

Jeshua inhaled every detail. "Perfect." He tied the reins to the short hitching post attached to his side of the wagon. "Hobble the mules for me. Their fetters are underneath the bench. Behind your feet."

Addan grabbed the fetters then climbed down from the wagon. He still felt lousy even though his headache was gone.

Jeshua did not wait for Addan. He walked up the hill and approached the three crosses.

Addan could not hear what was said between Jeshua and the guard as he hobbled the mules, but the tone of their verbal exchange seemed friendly. By the time Addan finished his task and reached the top of the hill, Jeshua was standing before Azriel.

A woman, wrapped in a rich but disheveled cloak, slept near the foot of Azriel's cross. Her face and head were covered; her dormancy made her look like a bundle of wet laundry.

Jeshua pointed at the bundle. "Who's that, I wonder?"

Addan bit his lower lip. "That might be his woman."

"You think so?"

"He does have one. A tough one, too."

"I would expect that from a man like him." Jeshua studied the unconscious man.

Azriel was broad and muscular and tempered as hard as steel. But the ravages of torture had mutilated his body and had broken his bones. The Galilean's massive head was covered with a thick black semi-long mane of hair and a full beard that was matted with clots of blood and dirt; body hair covered his back and chest and legs and arms. He was a hairy beast that had been treated as one. His broken legs were off-angled and grotesquely swollen.

Jeshua turned away from Azriel to study the other executed man, Nikos.

The young dead Greek lacked all body hair except under his arms and on his genitalia. What was left of his skin that was undamaged by the lash was as smooth as a woman's, including his bald face that possessed refined features. The hair on his head was fine and light brown, long and straight and matted into multiple clumps of clotted blood. He was short and slender, broken and dead. Other than validating what he had seen of past crucifixions, the young Greek offered Jeshua no new visual knowledge that he could use to terrify his audiences.

He turned to Azriel again.

This brute had potential. "Yes. Yes," Jeshua whispered.

Addan misinterpreted the pragmatic tone in Jeshua's whisper for that of sympathy. He studied the hairy beast.

Azriel's agonized and battered face was covered with a matted veil of wet and stringy hair. The stench of blood and decay drew flies and gnats and a variety of other insects. His wrists and ankles were nailed to the wood.

A wave of pain attacked the semi-conscious Azriel, forcing his torso to writhe like a damaged snake. His feet and hands twitched uncontrollably within their limited range of motion as if disassociated from their respective limbs. The intensified agony of his condition forced him to open his eyes. He cried. "Dinah! Dinah! Woman. Where are you if you've chosen to be here!? Dinah! Woman! What good are you!?"

Dinah stirred from her exhaustion—not slumber. She was too weak to speak or rise or continue to weep. Her hardened eyes softened when she gazed at her Azriel.

Gashes and bruising, grime and blood and matted hair covered his entire body. Birds of prey had already tried to pluck out his eyes or probe inside his ears. His mouth was a dry crack of agony that could not fully express the pain he was suffering.

The same pain that brought him closer to consciousness, closer to vagabond agony. Stray dissonant notes of misery projected from the back of his horribly parched throat and dissipated across the empty and barren place of the skull.

Azriel had been forced to straddle a rough and bloody wooden peg that extended from the lower portion of the stake. The weight of his body pressed unmercifully against his genitalia and the pain of the cuts and blisters in that region of the body prevented him from successfully shifting his weight to search for a moment of relief.

Azriel opened his feverish right eye; his left had been pecked at by birds and was swollen shut. "Curse these flies!" The interior of his dry mouth was cracked and blistered.

Dinah finally found the strength to rise. Her thick, wet cloak weighed heavily on her shoulders and across her back. She stumbled. Her mantle fell to her shoulders and exposed her hair and face; she did not bother to adjust the garment and raise it over her head. She approached Jeshua. "Who are you? What do you want?"

Jeshua acknowledged the aggressive woman and noted her hard beauty. But before he could respond to her, Azriel unleashed a harsh series of curses directed at her. She calmly withstood his insults and waited for exhaustion to prevail upon him.

Azriel exhaled weariness then sobbed. "Useless barren woman."

"I'm here, darling. I'm here, my love."

Jeshua considered this tough, no-nonsense woman who was being true to her man to the very end.

She was a mature woman with a plump and buxom figure—a handsome woman with steady eyes, balanced features, and a clear complexion. Her exposed braided hair was thick and long and brown. She was too exhausted to reach for the sides of her wet cloak to wrap it around her fitted tunic, which had a rich blaze of embroidery running along the edge of her collar.

"What are you looking at?" Dinah demanded. "This is not a freak show." Jeshua's lack of response further antagonized her. She pressed him for an answer. "You look like a slick one. Watch out for him, boy. He's a snake."

Addan was surprised that she had acknowledged his existence.

Azriel gazed down and focused his good eye upon Jeshua, who peered upward at Azriel: Their dark souls knew each other immediately.

Azriel struggled for his breath. "The world can . . . can never be . . . be rid of us." His wince meant to be a chuckle. "Never plead guilty." He coughed up blood. "Spit in their eye." Blood trickled from the right corner of his mouth.

Jeshua nodded. "I'm not Rabbi Jesus."

"Right." Azriel hacked. "Bah. Lunatic. Mystic."

Dinah's present invisibility became apparent to her.

Jeshua grinned.

His grin frightened her. Dissolved her defiance. Neutralized her aggression. She stepped away from Jeshua. Her eyes darkened with fear as she whispered, "Snake." She peered at her Azriel without fully turning away from Jeshua. "Death will come soon, my darling." She grimaced. "Death is here." Dinah shuddered.

Azriel groaned.

Addan trembled.

Jeshua devoured the sights and sounds and smells of Azriel and Dinah and Golgotha with detachment.

CHAPTER 11

Distance

Addan watched Golgotha recede into the increasing distance as Jeshua drove the wagon toward Damascus Gate. "You frightened her back there. You frightened me, too."

Jeshua ignored him.

Addan leaned over the side of the wagon to catch a final glance at the distant crosses. A bump in the road forced him to tighten his grip on the forward rib of the wagon's canopy to keep from falling out. "What happened?" He leaned back into the wagon with the aid of his right hand, which held onto the wagon's forward rib. He sat upright on the bench. "What happened back there?"

Jeshua flicked the reins at the mules. "Don't ask. You're not ready for an answer."

Addan bit his lower lip and stared at the mules. "Did you know him?"

"I said, don't ask."

Addan felt the increase in Golgotha's distance.

CHAPTER 12

Marketplace

Damascus Gate was an arched stone structure that was one of several gates that led into Jerusalem. There were two stone towers on either side of the broad arch that extended above the entranceway's edifice. The dual tower-and-gate structure was also wider and taller than both the adjoining city walls that extended in opposite directions and continued as a part of the large fortifying barrier that surrounded the city.

Traffic into and out of Jerusalem was heavy. Carts and wagons, burdened pedestrians, and beasts of burden traveled steadily through the gate in both directions.

Numerous impoverished porters carrying huge loads on their backs approached the city's gate like ants marching toward a puddle of honey. The humbleness of their appearance, however, could not conceal the dignity in their effort toward making a living.

On the back of one of these porters, there were eight clay pots tied to a wide backpack-board. A single length of rope wove around the pots' necks, over their large bodies, and through their closed-looped handles until a haphazard looking net was formed, which held the pots securely onto the wooden board. The man was forced to stoop forward to balance this load on his back. He had ropes looped under both arms to help keep the wooden device in place. And there was a rope that ran across the top of the wide board above his shoulders that he held up with both hands to keep the backpack-board balanced. The bulky load on his back seemed terribly heavy. Even the stoicism in the porter's eyes could not conceal the demands of his burden. His overly mended tunic, which came to his knees, was clean but extremely threadbare. A length of cloth was wrapped around his head to keep perspiration from rolling down into his eyes, and to protect his head from the elements of the early morning cold or from the midday heat or from another event of rain.

A heavily packed donkey led by a hard-eyed master approached their wagon from the opposite direction. The donkey was so heavily dressed with sacks and saddlebags that only his head and hooves could be seen. Neither the man nor the beast glanced in their direction as they passed the wagon.

Not far behind, a nomadic trader was riding a camel laden with a variety of items that were purchased to use for trade elsewhere—perhaps with those living in the desert wilderness or with those living in a remote village near the desert where rare goods would command a profitable price.

Jeshua's contentment grew as he watched the nomad ride by. "Everybody has got to make a living, my boy."

Merchants and nomads with their packed camels seemed everywhere, from everywhere: from the highways of the Northern region of Galilee and places beyond, like Egypt and Syria, and from the Southern regions of Judea and places beyond, like the desert and the westward sea—from everywhere and from nowhere merchants and nomads and pilgrims funneled into and poured out of Jerusalem's Damascus Gate.

Jeshua drove his wagon across the short bridge leading into the arched gate, then navigated through the deep tunnel that was as long as the width of the dual tower-and-gate structure.

The sun seemed brighter on the other side of the gate where a public marketplace, many times larger than any local neighborhood or village marketplace, unfolded before them.

Addan was intrigued by seeing this market through Jeshua's opportunistic eye. He was also excited by the market's sounds: merchants shouting at prospective customers, buyers haggling and bargaining and disputing endlessly with vendors, craftsmen such as coppersmiths and carpenters tapping and chipping at their work with hammers, crying fishmongers and shouting butchers competing with each other, bleating sheep and braying donkeys and whinnying horses and snorting camels and clucking foul standing nervously about. He was stimulated by the sights of foreign caravans, of the endless array of stalls and displays of raw grains and baked bread, of wineskins and water-filled goat skins, of fish and poultry, of spices sold by merchants sitting behind their large variety of individually prepared bags ready for sale. He was assaulted by the smells of grilling chicken and fish and locust, of baking bread and cakes, of simmering soups and stews. Everywhere he looked there were booths and tables, permanent shops and temporary tents, carts and wagons—all filled with merchandise or produce or livestock.

Everywhere Addan looked he formed a strong impression, which gave way to a new impression every few feet. The primary image of each vendor's shop that he saw blended into the next primary image, like a row of primary colors on a painter's palette being blended from one color to the next to form a secondary hue without forgetting the previous primary color and despite the growing number of secondary hues in his mind. The shops and booths and stalls blended with each other to contribute to the overall blur of organized public confusion as Jeshua's wagon traveled deeper into Damascus Gate's marketplace. The surrounding loud and colorful fluidity subdued Addan's shadowed memory of Golgotha's dark and silent finality. In fact, the noise of the marketplace was a relief; it distracted him from the nervous chatter inside his head that kept warning him to beware, to be more careful about—

"Wonderful!"

Addan was startled by Jeshua's first remark since they passed through Damascus Gate.

"We're almost too late." Jeshua peered at Addan as he flicked the reins gently at the mules.

His eyes had begun to sparkle again. "This place might be more lucrative than I thought. Hold on, Addan, this is going to be an interesting ride."

Addan welcomed this first kind utterance from Jeshua since Golgotha.

What was this effect Golgotha had on anyone who went there? Everyone who stepped foot upon its ground seemed to change in some inexplicable way: illumined by its darkness; darkened by its emptiness; shaken by its unintelligible yet captivating mystery.

Addan stole a glance at Jeshua.

How had Jeshua changed? Or had he been illumined so that Addan could see his true nature—or whatever it was he thought he saw—which left him feeling uneasy, yet drawn to him still. Drawn to a kind of danger that was both thrilling and life threatening. Yes, life threatening.

Addan's heart fluttered lightly. He took a deep breath to compensate for the discomfort.

What was he doing with Jeshua? And why couldn't he stop being with this strange and captivating man who drew him toward some kind of . . . of what?

Addan bit his lower lip.

Evil.

D. S. Lliteras

Addan shuddered. The chatter inside his head irritated him. Addan forced himself to stop thinking by immersing his senses into the depths of the chaotic marketplace surrounding him. His eyes and ears were flooded by what he saw and heard.

A man chased two scavenging dogs away from his fruit stand. He threw a rotten apricot at one of the skittish creatures. "Get away from here, you stinking mongrels!"

Older boys played ball in the east corner of the marketplace while younger children played tag and numerous other games closer to their parents' stands.

Some infants slept or cried, others nursed underneath their mothers' loose fitting tunics. Little girls played with dolls and teased each other.

A woman bent over a display of fruit and reached for a pomegranate. She had a round basket balanced on her head. The basket was wide and shallow, and its narrow rim kept her morning's shopping from falling out. She had another wicker basket, similar to the one on her head, tucked under her right arm. The family she was shopping for must have been very large. She glanced at a basket of melons with the pomegranate in her hand. She

103

decided against both of them, replaced the pomegranate, then moved on to another fruit stand.

An emaciated man, with bony legs and arms as
thin as a pair of upper branches in a winter tree,
extended his right arm with the palm of its hand facing upward to indicate his plea for alms. His social
status appeared to be lower than a beggar and his
health seemed to be poorer than a man on his
deathbed. The man sat like a cross-legged spider on
a frayed and tattered mat. He was too weak to raise
his head to acknowledge a copper's worth of gen-
erosity. The shoulder of his tunic on his left side was
torn away, leaving his corresponding chest, back,
shoulder, and arm exposed: He seemed to be on the
verge of leprosy and, in fact, may have already been
infected, but a heavy coat of dirt on his skin, along
with the maintenance of a safe distance from him by
most passersby, prevented any conclusive diagno-
sis. His threadbare mantle was held in place by a rag
tied around his head, which made him appear to be
wearing a soft-cover hat. The beggar man was so
weak that he leaned against the lower portion of a
crude walking stick, which he held erect with his
palsied left hand to keep himself seated upright.

The street was littered with men and women
immersed in deep poverty. So many, in fact, that

they were either invisible or ignored by the prosperous and the wealthy.

A cloth canopy extended over the entire front exterior of a weaver's workshop, including the shop's doublewide entranceway. Hanging from the rafters of the cloth canopy's frame was a makeshift hammock, where an infant slept. The hammock was made from a colorfully woven piece of fabric: an imperfect remnant, an unmarketable discard, a flawed or leftover portion from a larger sheet that would be commonly available in any weaver's home. A length of rope was tied to each knotted corner of the hammock remnant and tied to the corresponding rafter above.

A mother nearby kept a watchful eye on the baby. She placed the palm of her hand against the baby's rump and gave it a gentle push to keep the hammock swinging and, therefore, keep the baby asleep. Nobody noticed this small feminine act—not even the mother herself.

"Look at those vendors," said Jeshua. "Marvelous. And already present in great numbers." He was ecstatic. "How wonderfully crazy. Look, over there: holy water for sale. Water from a well your rabbi messiah drank from. Splendid! And look, there: Messiah thorns, two shekels for those stained with his blood and one shekel for those without his blood. Very good. Very imaginative. Very enterprising." He peered at Addan with the glassy eyes of a winning gambler. "It looks as if your derelict rabbi is not forgotten after all. At least, not in the marketplace. Marvelous. This is looking more lucrative than my first impression. This is really something. Yes, like I said, this is going to be a wild and interesting ride."

"You think so?"

"Can't you see this wonderful carnival around us? They're already selling his magic. They're already coming as close to paganism as they can—as they dare. I love it. Oh, Jerusalem, Jerusalem, city of the world." Jeshua enthusiastically flicked the reins at the mules.

Addan was disturbed by what Jeshua was enthusiastic about in this marketplace.

Holy water. Messiah thorns. Splinters from his cross. Threads from his robe.

Addan felt queasy. And sad.

The idea of Rabbi Jesus being further abused and exploited after his death had been inconceivable to him. That is, until now.

Addan looked in one direction, then another.

What was he doing? What was he trying to prove? And who was this man he was sitting next to?

Addan turned away from the hucksters and the magicians and sought comfort through familiar sights.

Through a narrow alleyway, one of several that fed into the marketplace like their corresponding streets, Addan caught a glimpse of a squatting mother bathing her child in a large clay bowl that was wide enough to serve as a tub. The sleeves of her tunic were rolled up her arms above their elbows, the mantle covering her head was pulled away from her face and draped over her back, and the hem of her tunic came up to the calves of her legs, exposing her bare feet and ankles. The contented child splashed water on his mother.

Addan turned away from the mother and child and peered into the general marketplace.

A crowd of women were studying three rows of short tables that were roughly aligned on the west side of the marketplace: some with and some without temporary canopies to provide a little shade. In all directions of the market, abundance could be seen.

Pomegranates and apricots, figs and dates were being sold by one vendor. Walnuts, almonds, and pistachios were being sold by another. Numerous men were selling grain, which included barley and millet, wheat and rye. A woman at one table displayed pots of cinnamon and cumin, mint and mustard. All along the west side there were grains and vegetables and fruit; figs and dates, apricots and apples.

Toward the center of the market there were several men who tended a pair of two-wheeled carts that were partially unloaded to display the variety of wood they had for sale: cedar and cypress, ash and oak, pine and ebony and fir. Only in a city the size of Jerusalem could such a variety be found.

Rich and poor vendors stood side by side trying to make a living. One vendor sold luxury items, and another sold salt. One man hawked aloe and frankincense, and another man begged and implored.

There was a double archway that revealed the ground floor interior of a two-story abode that sold wine by the skin, as well as by the cup; several men who were already drunk stood inside the area that operated as a tavern.

Rich and poor shoppers wandered about, either purchasing what they could afford or stealing what they could get away with.

Chickens clucked. Babies cried. Shoppers haggled with vendors. Various merchants announced:

"Milk and yogurt."

"Cheese and eggs."

"Wine and vinegar."

"Lamps and fans."

Addan devoured the sights and sounds of the Damascus Gate market and pushed aside his concerns over Jeshua's character, his own questionable behavior and intentions, and his sorrow over Jesus' death.

"You're acting as if you've never been here before," said Jeshua.

"I find Damascus Gate exciting."

"Yes. Yes. I can understand that." Jeshua studied the beautiful bedlam of trade. "This marketplace is a lot larger than I thought it was going to be."

"It's the largest in the Second Quarter."

"I see. What do you know about this place?"

"Well. Many of those who come here are foreigners."

"I can see that."

"Yes. Well. And . . . and although most Jerusalemites shop for their fruits and vegetables at their neighborhood markets, they also like to frequent Damascus Gate to seek out whatever coarse entertainment is available to break the monotony of relentless work."

"Well, well. Why didn't you tell me this sooner?"

"You were too busy telling me."

Jeshua was so surprised by Addan's answer that he brought the mules to a halt. "You—you have real potential, boy." He warmly slapped Addan on the back. "You got me, boy. And believe me, that's a rare thing." Jeshua scanned his surroundings enthusiastically. "So. What's near this Second Quarter?"

"The Tyropoeon Valley."

"What is that?"

"It's where the upper classes live. Over there. In that direction."

"Is that right?" Jeshua said thoughtfully.

"What?"

"I smell gold and copper. I smell the rich, as well as the poor." He grinned at Addan.

"But for the most part, it is servants and slaves who come here—"

"For the fat and lazy upper classes, my boy, who are always bored and hungry and looking for some form of entertainment to occupy their stupid and idle minds. But their servants and slaves can't enjoy that for them. No way. Hmm. Yes. Hedonists. Gluttons. All of them." Jeshua ignored the bewildered expression etched across Addan's face and inhaled the fullness of his surroundings instead.

"Hello, Second Quarter. The Master of Secrets is here."

Addan was infected by Jeshua's enthusiasm despite his bafflement. "What now?"

"There. Over there is where we will set up the wagon."

"Why not by the tavern?"

"That's too close to my direct competition."

"Direct?"

"I'm selling potions. They're selling wine. Where would you spend your meager shekel?—perhaps, even your last."

"I see what you mean. Still—"

"I know. We're still not that far from them to make a difference, but that's an illusion. Especially when it concerns an audience."

"An audience?"

"That's right. Remember. I'm running a business here. I'm selling magic as well as potions. Any distance from my audience, as well as from that tavern, increases my magic's power. Distance increases the illusion."

"You speak as if you don't believe in magic at all."

"Magic is for children and believers."

"Believers of what?"

Jeshua pointed toward the center of the market-place where the firewood vendors were setting up their stand. "Over there."

"Where?"

"Beside that boring pile of wood."

"Believers of what?"

Jeshua winked. "That's good positioning. There's no competition with dead wood." He chuck-led, handed Addan the reins, and jumped off the wagon.

Addan was captivated by Jeshua's flamboy-ance. This softened the uneasiness he always felt over Jeshua's puzzling statements and his unan-swered questions.

Jeshua strolled in front of Beba. He grabbed the mule's halter to lead her in order to bring the wagon to the exact spot he wanted to set up his humble platform that served as a theatrical stage.

"Tie off the reins," Jeshua commanded.

Addan whipped the reins twice around the wagon's hitching post then looped the working end of the reins around the taut length of the reins that led to the mules before tying them off. Then he jumped off the wagon, stretched his legs, and peered toward the southerly side of the market square where there was another row of permanent workshops that housed tradesmen and their wares.

An open pair of solid doors set within an arched entranceway revealed the interior of a dark workshop where a heavily bearded man wearing a round cap sat on a low bench, bent over his work. With a small hammer, the craftsman tapped on the head of a steel punch as he guided its point against the surface of a copper pot. Tap tap. Tap tap. Tap tap. He applied himself with the attentiveness and the loving care of a true craftsman who was creating a work of art. His entranceway was open to the marketplace square in order to encourage passersby to stop and appreciate his skills, as well as to encourage the shoppers to examine his display of finely designed copperware. Tap tap. Tap tap. Tap tap.

A weaver displayed numerous rugs, as well as rolls of cloth used to make garments. Some fabrics were intricately woven and expensively dyed with rich hues; other fabrics were plainly woven and inexpensively homespun for those who could not afford to purchase color. Inside the dim recesses of the workshop stood a large vertical loom. Three women worked quietly together to weave a fine woolen fabric.

A heavily bearded shoemaker with serious eyes sat straddled on his bench and bent over a half-built leather sandal fitted over an upside-down wooden foot that was attached to one end of a thick rod; the other end was affixed to the work bench. He was one of many tradesmen who could be found crowded into the periphery of this marketplace and along the Second Quarter's streets working in their dimly lit street-front shops inside the first floor of their city dwellings. He shaved a strip of leather off one side of the heel with a sharp implement; there were a variety of tools strewn on the floor by his feet.

Jeshua nudged Addan's side with his elbow. "Well, we can't stand here all morning gawking at the sights."

Addan glanced to his left and saw an oxen-drawn cart laden with roughly cut firewood being driven toward them at the center of the marketplace where there was a double pile of firewood already stacked up behind the place Jeshua had parked the wagon. The firewood merchants were obviously expecting a lively business due to the dampness of the weather and the persistent chill of the night.

The two-wheeled cart plodded ponderously toward its destination. The solid wheels were made of slats of wood that were joined by tongue-and-groove and held together by a parallel pair of wooden cross braces above and below the axle hole. The wooden braces were pegged into slots to hold the wheel solidly together. The cart's bed had three posts on either side: a front, middle, and rear post, which served to keep the stack of wood from falling off the cart. The pair of oxen dragged and the primitive cart creaked from the heavy load of firewood.

"You need to stop gawking, yourself," said Addan.

Jeshua laughed with great pleasure at Addan's growing defiance. "I'm planning, my boy. I'm not merely enjoying the potential of this carnival."

"I see."

"That you will."

A man approached them from the other side of the double stack of firewood at the center of the marketplace. He was a rough-looking sort.

Both men disliked each other immediately.

"Look out there," the man commanded.

"Look out, yourself," Jeshua countered, as he approached the rear of his wagon.

"I'm in charge of the wood vending stand on the other side of these firewood stacks."

"All right. I'm in charge of this wagon."

"Then move it. You're wagon is sitting on the place were I was going to set up my second stand."

Jeshua ignored the surly man. Instead, he stood with his back facing the rear of the wagon as he studied the panorama of the marketplace and its carnival atmosphere. He addressed Addan. "We have a perfect view of the gate from here. Therefore, they have a perfect view of us. Perfect."

The angry firewood vendor grumbled then strode behind the larger of the two firewood piles.

Jeshua winked at Addan. "We are in sight of the flow of traffic. That will bring us a constantly changing audience. Beautiful."

"I don't think that firewood vendor appreciates our squatting here."

"Don't worry about him. He'll change his tune as soon as he starts benefiting from the business we draw to this vicinity of the market. You'll see."

But the angry leader of the firewood vendors and two of his tribe were not prepared to wait for Jeshua to demonstrate his future benefit to them. As they approached Jeshua, each of them brandished a length of wood from their pile to indicate that they were prepared to use them as weapons.

"Addan. Take hold of Beba's halter. Go on. Keep the mules still."

"Be careful, Jeshua."

"Go on, I said. Hold the mules steady."

Addan hustled to the heads of both mules and grabbed their halters as Jeshua turned toward the approaching men and awaited their arrival.

"You're occupying our space," said the leader.

"You're already set up on the other side," said Jeshua.

"I told you I was planning to set up a second stand on this side as well."

"Well. I'm here now," said Jeshua.

"You're not from around here," said the leader.

"No." Jeshua made a show of studying his surroundings. "And I don't see many people around here who are."

The leader took a threatening step toward Jeshua. "You're not going to stay here."

Jeshua took a threatening step toward him. "Yes, I am."

The leader swung the club at Jeshua, who ducked beneath the arc of its path. Jeshua countered with a hard right into the man's side with his fist. The leader dropped to his knees from the wicked punch. Jeshua grabbed the disabled man's club and parried the swing of another club.

The second man's club splintered loudly, which startled the man. He retreated a step and looked at the third man who was bewildered at first, then considered attacking.

"Don't," said Jeshua.

The third man didn't.

Jeshua peered at their leader who was still on his knees, breathless and aching from the blow; his left arm was wrapped around the lower portion of his chest.

"I'm here to stay. Do you understand?"

The leader rose unsteadily. "You'll pay for this as well." He grimaced. "Yes. I remember you. I haven't forgotten you, mister."

"Ahh. You've elevated my social standing already."

The man did not appreciate Jeshua's humor. "Fine. There's time." He waved his free hand at the other two. "There's plenty of time." The leader turned away from Jeshua and strode away immersed in a hateful contemplation. The other two followed without saying a word.

Jeshua peered at Addan as soon as the men disappeared behind their firewood mounds. "What do you think?"

"You're crazy," said Addan, as he released the mules' halters and approached Jeshua. "Does he know you?"

"You held the mules."

"They did not need holding. They already know their master's habits."

Jeshua laughed then flung the length of wood into the nearby woodpile.

CHAPTER 13

Performance

Eleven burning torches surrounded the stage-platform where Jeshua stood. The torchlights created long and uncertain shadows that danced into different positions whenever the evening's wind veered. Just below the seat of each torch's flame the wood sweated resin. Above the fire seats, the oil-soaked cloth that was wrapped around the head of each torch caused the wood to smoke and pop and, occasionally, throw sparks into the air.

The fire of these crude footlights pushed the night behind those in the audience who were huddled close to the stage-platform. Those who stood at a greater distance from the performance area blended into the general surrounding darkness and stood either within or near the deep and black and engulfing pockets of space.

Addan quickly learned how to disappear within these pockets. He enjoyed the power of being visible in the light while beating a small drum that Jeshua had taught him to use in order to help draw an audience and, thereafter, keep them excited. He also enjoyed becoming invisible whenever he stepped into a deep pocket and ceased drumming, which is where he was at this moment.

Invisible. Nervous. Afraid. Almost as if he'd been struck dumb.

He peered at Jeshua, who was successfully holding the audience's attention and who no longer needed the beat of his drum. Addan held the small drum with both hands to conceal a nervousness so intense that he could not comprehend what Jeshua was saying.

Jeshua looked bigger than he actually was; he looked huge on stage. His presence and charm had increased immeasurably. His melodic voice had lulled everybody into listening to him. Somehow, he made everybody feel as if he were their friend, as if he were one of them. But he was not.

He was well nourished. Well dressed. Well groomed. Refined. Almost regal in manner and appearance. It was as if the stage had transformed him into something more than he was: Jesus, son of

Shallum—whoever that was. You simply could not take your eyes off him on that feebly lit stage-platform.

Jeshua had removed his mantle to show off his thick shoulder-length hair. This seemed to appeal to some of the women in the audience.

A bird suddenly appeared in Jeshua's hand and caused the audience to stir with pleasure. And when he released the bird into the night, the audience gasped with delight then openly approved with a short applause.

Addan grew calmer with the crowd's growing warmth. He began to hear The Master of Secrets. And then—over there—he saw. On the placard. Against the backstage curtain that closed off the rear of the wagon and concealed its interior. Behind Jeshua and below the other placard that said "Healing Tonics for Sale," the lower placard said in Greek and Latin, Hebrew and Aramaic: "The Master of Secrets."

Jeshua had a yellow stoppered vial in one hand and a red stoppered vial in the other. He presented them with a flourish of words and gestures that were mesmerizing even to Addan, who knew what Jeshua was doing.

Jeshua slipped from Aramaic into Hebrew, uttered a few words in Latin, then jumped into Greek and back-flipped into Aramaic whenever he found it necessary. He managed to find a commonality in the language that his entire audience could understand—an audience comprised of people who comprehended a smattering of all these languages, but who were not necessarily fluent in them all. Most importantly, Jeshua managed to find the humor that existed in each of these languages as well as in between the languages. His true genius was his ability to find his audience's collective tongue—then reach deeply into their linguistic understanding and tap into their well of humor and find the flow of their laughter.

Once Jeshua understood their source of laughter, he ventured into storytelling and testimonials, which led to the sale of his potions. It was a slow and subtle process that seemed natural because, by this time, everybody was his friend. He could be trusted. And his potions—well—that wasn't magic. That's what the bird was for. His potions were now bona fide cures—at least, according to those audience members who parted with their hard earned copper and—

Addan saw the purse dangling from the man's leather belt.

There. Ahead.

Addan released his right hand from the drum, but held the drum close to his chest with his left in order to conceal what he was about to do with his right. He stepped out of the dark pocket and carefully weaved past two layers of the crowd toward the stage-platform.

There was another dark pocket near the man.

Addan eased into the space like any invisible child could do. He peered at Jeshua, who caught his glance. Jeshua somehow managed to remind Addan to keep focused on what he was doing; to concentrate, or he'd be caught—all this Jeshua conveyed in a single glance.

Addan heard Jeshua's voice intensify as he studied the man's purse:

Fat. Very fat. And open at the top. It would not be difficult to spread the neck of the already partially open purse and reach inside it.

Addan noted a discarded clay vial on the ground by the man's feet.

Ahh. A moment of carelessness. Disarmed by laughter. Eased by the purchase of the potion. Relaxed by the crowd's warmth. And now, because the man was lost in a moment of reverie, of well-being, he had forgotten to pull tight the cords of his leather purse.

Addan eased closer to the man. He looked up at Jeshua who caught his glance again and managed to convey to Addan that he understood where Addan was. Then Addan thought he heard Jeshua say: "Where are you?" But Jeshua knew where he was. Jeshua knew! So, "what are you" had to be closer in meaning to what Jeshua was asking. And "what are you" was the question that reverberated inside Addan's head as he reached into the man's purse and drew out a small handful of what felt like denarii.

The crowd erupted into a huge roar of laughter.

The man with the purse startled Addan when he bent forward with a chortle that added to the rollick and the cheers of the many in the audience.

Addan concealed the fist full of denarii behind the drum and concealed his success at becoming a thief. He glanced up at Jeshua, who glanced down at him from the stage-platform.

Addan's success had not escaped Jeshua's attention. Jeshua's eyes, those eyes, shined with approval as he continued with his performance as if nothing were being shared between him and Addan.

Oddly, Addan drew comfort from those eyes. Uneasily, he needed them.

Addan felt weak at the knees. He wanted to be sick. But those eyes wouldn't let him. They followed him to the next purse. And the next. Until those eyes were not necessary. Until Addan finally understood the thrill, the invincibility, the joy, the sin of this danger that could not be explained to anybody who had not experienced it. He filled the inside of the drum with copper and silver. And as he filled up the drum he emptied himself of fear and of . . . of what? What?

CHAPTER 14

Thieves

The crack of the morning light caught Addan's attention. He peered through the vertical separation between the wagon's rear curtain and the side of the wagon's canopy. He noticed that the intensity of the sun caused the costly goods that were displayed upon a table, as well as upon a couple of ground mats, to twinkle for attention. These displays were out in the open and in front of another table that sat underneath a permanent portico, which offered more of the same kind of expensive merchandise. The sun intensified the value and emphasized the delicacy of the items that the merchant had to offer. Gold necklaces and silver bracelets. Blown-glass bottles and vases. Bottles of perfume and precious oils. Highly decorated oil lamps. Expensively dyed fabrics. Local and imported goods that were generally found only in a market this size and within a city quarter as wealthy as the Second Quarter district of Jerusalem near Damascus Gate. Numerous matrons and their servants gathered around these tables and ground mats to inspect and verify the quality of what the merchant had to offer.

Addan leaned against the rear of the driver's bench and against the curtain that closed off the front of the wagon. He stretched his legs in an effort to maximize a moment of relaxation as he nested comfortably on the chest that sat in the forward left side of the wagon's bed. Addan enjoyed the temporary safety of this privacy as he continued to study the bright marketplace from the relatively dark interior of the wagon. The gentle clinking of pottery drew his attention away from the chink of reality outside and toward the subdued activity inside.

Jeshua was placing a number of miniature clay vials into a large and colorfully decorated wooden box. The wooden stoppers of the miniature vials were wrapped with differently colored pieces of fabric. Some had a white piece of cotton cloth, some had a strip of brown woolen fabric, and others had red-colored linen. Three colors. White, brown, and red; cotton, wool, and linen.

Jeshua addressed Addan as if he'd been reading the boy's thoughts. "I charge more money for the red vials. To the eye of most buyers, red is always more expensive."

Addan sat up straight in order to look down into the box. "But you said yourself that there's not anything of value in them."

"Materially, my boy. Materially." He held up one of the red-stoppered vials with his right hand and pointed to himself with his left index finger. "The value lies within my customer's anticipation. His expectation. His need. Most of all, his belief in the power of potions. The power—dare I say?—the power of magic." He placed the red-stoppered vial into the box.

"What are you doing?"

"I'm getting ready for our second show. Last night's performance was very successful." He winked at Addan. "You did very well." Jeshua grabbed the small drum that Addan used last night and shook it. "Really well." He opened one of the large chests. "You're a natural." He reached inside the chest, unhooked the latches on both sides of a small box, and raised the box's lid. Then he released a latch on the side of the drum, opened a tiny door, and poured the coins from the drum into the box.

"Are you going to count it?"

"What's the point? The amount is what it is." Jeshua closed the money box, latched the lid, and slammed the trunk shut. "You did good."

"I . . . I guess I did—good."

Jeshua ignored Addan's guilty tone. "I like to start with an evening show first when I arrive at a new location."

"Why?"

"Because the lower classes and those outcasts of the underworld are more likely to come. And they're the people I gladly understand. Our kind of people. But more importantly, if we can steal successfully from our own kind in an unfamiliar locale, then we can successfully steal from the softer upper classes living in the same locale. Not only that. If we happen to get caught, I can always talk my way out of it with those of the lower classes who have a greater understanding for the need to steal. They are often capable of laughing it off after recovering their money, and after having a drink on me. The upper classes, however, are another matter entirely."

"I see."

"We did well last night. My audience tested well. Now, I need to teach you how to operate during the day—and against the not so generous wealthier upper classes, who are more careful about their money."

"Which means, they are also more dangerous."

"Precisely. You're a smart boy."

"I'm not so sure about that."

Jeshua ignored the boy's insecurity. "And another thing. Daytime audiences are generally edgier and are more apt to steal from me."

"You?"

"Sure." He looked at his vials. "That's why I don't like to have a large number of these on stage. Once I get started, once the spirit gets a hold of me, look out. You already know I can perform like a demon." He reached for several brown-stoppered vials. "And, when I'm on, I'm not always alert. Vials are often stolen from me when I'm in this vulnerable state."

Addan plucked a dried fig from one of the nearby food baskets. "Should I keep my eye on them during your performance?"

"No, no. Never accuse a thief. No. We don't want to draw attention to what we are doing ourselves."

"We." Addan nervously chewed into the fig and did not enjoy its sweetness.

"Yes. We. You're supposed to have a drum full of their money. It would not be very smart to get caught stealing by accusing somebody else of stealing."

"I see." Addan swallowed his mouthful of fig. "It's because——," he swallowed again, "because, I'd be drawing attention to myself."

"That's right. And any cry of theft into the crowd causes people to suddenly check their own purses. And when they find them to be lighter than they're supposed to be, it would not take long for them to realize that it was you who was standing near them at some point during the performance. And it would not take them long to seize and search you and your drum, as well, and proclaim you to be a thief."

"I see."

"Remember, these are people who are used to being with their own kind. They are basically distrustful toward anyone outside their tribe. They can smell an outsider, sense any intruder in their space—at least, they can surely remember the closeness of a stranger's presence when it comes to being robbed of their hard-earned money."

Addan shifted uneasily on the chest he was sitting on. "This is awfully dangerous to me."

"This is very dangerous work." Jeshua smiled broadly. "And I'm glad you're still up to it."

Addan sat up straight again and nibbled nervously on his lower lip. He liked Jeshua's approval and the confident tone in his voice. He liked the tension of conspiracy and the anticipated danger. God help him. He couldn't stop himself. He couldn't. "I can do it."

Jeshua stood up. His head hit one of the crystals. The inverted tree of dangling crystals bobbed and wobbled haphazardly in a chaotic orbit. He bowed his head in a startled response that forced him to glance upward.

An accident. At last. A misstep.

Jeshua glanced at Addan, averted his eyes, then approached the vertical chink of light in the rear of the wagon. He carefully pulled the curtain aside to widen his view of the marketplace. "I know you can. But for now, I'm simply going to be a hawker."

"A what?"

Something caught Jeshua's eye. "A seller of healing potions." He leaned toward the curtain in an effort to see better. "This is my way of testing the vulnerability of those who come to Damascus Gate." He held a quiet gaze for a long while. "Yes. She's beautiful. I'd like to—" He released the curtain and turned to Addan, "to measure the attitudes of those who live in the rich Second Quarter nearby. Every marketplace has its own personality and it alters the behavior of the pilgrims who visit."

"But this is Passover. The Festival of Unleavened Bread. Pilgrims from every corner of the Roman Empire will be coming here."

Jeshua sat on a small stool near the box he was packing vials into and began counting them. "One, two, three, four—And?—five, six, seven—And?"

"Well. With eight days of festival and so many different pilgrims entering Jerusalem to bring sacrifices to the Temple and to sell their merchandise, don't you think it is rather impossible to measure their behavior as a whole?"

"There's always a pattern, my boy. Eleven, twelve, thirteen. Patterns always develop. People always to want to fit in, even when they are outsiders, foreigners, pilgrims, merchants—whatever. There's always a pattern. Always. Nineteen, twenty, twenty-one. Do you understand? Do you?" Jeshua looked up from the vials he was counting to see if Addan was still listening.

Addan was struggling to get free from a powerful arm that was wrapped around his throat and an equally powerful hand with a very thick cloth pressed over his mouth to prevent him from screaming.

Before Jeshua could respond, a second man shoved him from behind so hard that he tumbled toward the boy in a forward somersault and crashed into baskets and pottery and almost hit his head on the corner of the chest that Addan had been sitting on. The wagon shuddered and creaked under his fallen weight. A clay pot shattered. The canopy bellowed. The inverted crystal trees above danced about frantically and clinked as some of them collided with each other.

Jeshua managed to rise and face his attacker—the leader of the firewood vendors.

The leader stood inside the rear entrance of the wagon. The backstage curtain had been drawn closed behind him. This time he was brandishing a black dagger in his right hand.

"Stop your struggling," commanded Addan's captor, "or I'll snap your neck in two."

Addan relaxed and looked on helplessly.

"So, we meet again," said the firewood leader to Jeshua."

"Do I know you?"

"I know it's been a long time. But don't try to pretend your way out of this."

"I don't know what you're talking about."

The firewood leader's lips twisted with rage. "You stole a season's worth of living from me."

"I don't steal."

"Your dice were crooked."

"I don't need that kind of help to take your money. I'm a skilled gambler and you're not."

"Then you do remember me."

"If you say so." Jeshua feigned boredom, which increased the firewood leader's anger.

"You cheated me!" The firewood leader struck Jeshua across the face with his open left hand.

Addan was shocked by the seriousness of this insult: as great an insult as one could express to another. His captor increased the pressure around his throat.

Jeshua backhanded the firewood leader across the mouth in response. Blood flowed from the right corner of the man's mouth.

The firewood leader wiped his mouth with the back of his left forearm and studied the blood. He seemed to enjoy the injury.

Addan's eyes widened. Blood feuds began with such an insult. Began with a few drops of blood. And often ended with death.

"This does not have to be a blood feud," Jeshua said.

The leader touched the right corner of his mouth. "It is now." He glowered at Addan. "I'm going to cut out both your hearts."

"You want this location? You can have it."

"You know damn well this is not about where your wagon is placed."

"Don't hurt the boy."

The man restraining Addan laughed.

"First you, then the boy," said the leader with an evil grin. "In that way, I leave no blood feud behind."

"The feud is of your creation. The boy is not mine."

The leader took a threatening step toward Jeshua. "You're not going to be able to talk your way out of this like your kind always does."

Jeshua stepped toward him in response.

The leader tightened his grip on the dagger's handle. "Trickster."

Addan began to struggle against his captor again.

As soon as the distracted firewood leader glanced in Addan's direction, Jeshua leaped toward his opponent and managed to grab the man's wrist to gain control of the dagger.

The leader was strong. His powerful arm was as unyielding as a thick, sturdy branch hanging from a hardwood tree.

Jeshua was surprised by the man's strength. Earlier, the man's lack of pugilistic agility caused Jeshua to underestimate the power and cunning of his dangerous opponent. He realized that the wagon's confinement provided a combat environment that his opponent was using to his tactical advantage.

Jeshua was forced to use both hands to restrain the right arm that wielded the dagger. He was thus forced to leave himself open to the man's vicious punch to his right side. This left him breathless. He hunched forward after the man's second blow. His knees buckled. His hands convulsed. His vision blurred.

The leader wrenched the dagger free and jabbed it into Jeshua's upper left arm.

Jeshua yelped.

The man pulled out the dagger and prepared to stab Jeshua again. But Jeshua jerked his knee into the man's groin and paralyzed him with excruciating pain that lasted long enough to connect a right cross to the man's jaw, which dazed him. The man dropped the dagger.

Jeshua ignored the growing pain in his upper left arm as he turned and struck the man's face with a backhand, then came around with a left hook to the gut, and followed through with a hard right across the jaw. He grabbed the man's head by his hair and slammed his face against the upper edge of the wagon's side. Blood spurted everywhere as the man fell to the floor unconscious.

"Look out, Jeshua!"

Jeshua reached for the dagger as he heard a crash. It was Addan being tossed aside. Jeshua turned around with the black dagger in his right hand and with his arm extended in defense just in time for Addan's former captor to accidentally impale himself in the abdomen as he lunged toward Jeshua. The man's eyes widened with terror equal to Jeshua's; they both knew this was fatal—for both of them.

Jeshua did not pull out the dagger when the man faltered, then weakened, then—he released the handle and took a step backward as the man dropped to his knees. The man reached for the handle of the dagger with both hands, lost his strength, and fell sideways to the wagon's bed. A single gasp preceded his death.

Jeshua swayed from side to side with exhaustion and bewilderment as he peered at the slaughtered beast at his feet.

A full and heavy beard, a thick and long head of hair, and a wild growth of hair covering his short arms and legs and stocky torso made the slain man look like a Syrian bear.

Addan struggled to his feet. "Jeshua. You're hurt."

Jeshua blinked like a beaten drunk. "Is he . . . is he dead?"

"I . . . I don't know."

Jeshua reached for his upper left arm and felt the wetness of his blood that already soaked through the upper sleeve of his tunic. "I'm hurt."

Addan stepped over broken pottery and shattered crystals, sidestepped strewn chests and boxes and baskets. Several of the inverted hanging trees were missing their crystals; others were dangling from broken and off-balanced sticks. The destruction of the canopy's magical sky mirrored the disarray in the wagon's interior below. Addan began to step over the man Jeshua had stabbed, but knelt beside him instead.

"Is he?"

Addan touched the man's chest. "He's not breathing. I don't feel his heartbeat." He pulled out the dagger. "Yes. I think he's dead."

"Hmm."

"What are we going to do?"

Jeshua nodded in the direction of the other man. "And that one?"

Addan stood up and approached the other man who was lying face down on the wagon's bed.

"Be careful. He's powerful. And mean."

There was a large puddle of blood near the man's head.

Addan carefully stooped over him and placed his trembling hand on the side of the man's neck.

"Well?"

"Wait." He grabbed the hair on the back of the man's head and gently lifted his face off the floor. Addan recoiled, dropping the dagger. "God." He involuntarily released the man's hair. The head thumped facedown on the wagon's bed.

"What?"

"His forehead is split open. His skull is broken." Addan looked up at Jeshua. "How did you—? He's dead."

Jeshua faltered in his attempt to step closer to verify Addan's assessment.

Addan hurried to his side and assisted him to one of the chests. The exhale that followed after Jeshua sat down expressed a feeling of doom.

Jeshua reached for his injured arm again and felt the saturation of his tunic's full-length sleeve. "I'm bleeding."

"He stuck you good."

"Yes." Jeshua grimaced. "Go on. Get out of here."

"Go?" Addan blinked his eyes hard. "Go where?"

"Save yourself. Run."

"I can't leave you now. You're hurt."

"I can take care of myself."

Addan pursed his lips. His eyes burned with determination. "I'm not going."

"Hmm." Jeshua nodded with approval. "You're a better assistant than I thought you were going to be."

"I don't know about that. I . . . I don't know about anything anymore. My world." Addan shook his head in an effort to hold back his tears. "My world is . . . is upside down and I'm . . . I'm here. With you." Addan studied the two dead men. "And now, there's blood between us."

"Yes." Jeshua nodded. "Blood can bind—men."

144

Addan lowered his gaze. "Well. . . ."

"Have you ever dressed a wound?"

"I've watched my mother tend to the sick and injured many times."

"Good. You've got to stop the bleeding."

"I'll . . . I'll try."

Jeshua glanced at the two dead men. "We've got to work fast."

Addan was suddenly terrified again. "How?"

"In that basket, there are washcloths and fabric. Get the waterskin as well. And . . . and the washbowl, yes, over there. It's not broken. Hurry." Jeshua frowned. "Don't just stand there like a lost child." He stressed his impatience with a pant. "Help me out of this tunic."

"But . . . but what are we going to do with them?"

"Them? Well." Jeshua exhaled forcefully then winced. "They're coming with us."

"Us?"

"We're getting out of here, boy."

"We are?"

"Yes. We are going to pack up like two successful thieves and ride out of here as if nothing happened."

"But—"

"Nothing happened. Now help me out of this tunic. I have another one in that chest over there. Hurry. Our lives depend on it."

CHAPTER 15

Rabbi

Jeshua was stripped down to his white linen loincloth. His tunic lay in a heap at his feet; its left sleeve was soaked with blood.

He hunched forward from where he sat, on the right rear chest near the driver's bench, and winced. Pain and concern intensified his brow.

His left arm was crossed loosely over his abdomen and his right arm was crossed rigidly over his chest so his right hand could apply direct pressure on the dagger wound to his upper left arm in order to slow down the bleeding. "Some people can't take a joke."

"Some joke," said Addan. "Some people don't like being cheated."

"Then the idiot shouldn't have gotten into the game."

"What kind of game?"

"Gambling. Not a game, really."

"You were gambling?"

"Yes. Of course. What do you think we've been talking about? And why the long face?"

Addan shook his head. "Gambling."

"Look. It's not my fault he couldn't throw winning dice."

"Gambling with dice? But . . . but dice are sacred."

"It even cost him his life."

"I'm not joking."

"Neither am I." Jeshua grimaced. "Am I going to sit here all afternoon pressing my hand against my bleeding arm or are you going to apply a bandage on it?"

"Sorry. Where—?"

"Over there. Where I told you. Wait. In that basket over there." Jeshua noted the confusion in Addan's face. "The basket that you loaded into the wagon yourself. Over there!"

"I'm sorry." Addan hustled to the basket and reached inside it where there were washcloths and lengths of linen.

"Bring the whole basket over here. I thought you said you'd watched your mother do this."

Addan lifted the basket from the wagon's floor and set it before Jeshua's feet. "I'm sorry."

"Snap out of it. There's no time for confusion. We're in too much trouble for that."

"I know." Addan took out a clean washcloth and a rolled strip of linen. "I know. You killed him—them—"

"No. It was in self-defense."

"That's right. It was not an accidental slaying."

"But . . . but in truth it was. Don't you think?"

"Don't try to convince me." Addan folded the small washcloth in half. "Convincing the judges is what you have to do."

"Hmm. You have something there. I suppose my defense before a court won't sound too convincing coming from the likes of me."

"Not from an entertainer." Addan folded the washcloth in half again, which reduced its size to a fourth of itself as well as thickened its blood absorbing capabilities by as many times. "Not from a man of amusement. Not from—"

"Right. All right. I get the point. Then . . . then I'll avoid them. I'll . . . I'll appeal to other judges."

Addan had Jeshua release his arm. He placed the bandage against the wound. "Press against this."

Jeshua held the bandage against his wound with his right hand. "What other judges?"

"At a refuge city." Jeshua seemed to confirm something within himself. "Yes, we're going to try and make it to a refuge city where an accused man, who is on the run from those seeking revenge, can stand a fair trial."

"That so-called refuge probably won't do you any good."

"Well—it's better than nothing. Better than trying to outrun that crazy lot of firewood vendors—or whatever they truly are."

"I don't know." Addan partially unrolled the linen strip. He pushed away Jeshua's hand and removed the bandage momentarily. "This wound looks serious." He replaced the bandage, pressed the working end of the roll against it, and unwound the entire linen roll over the bandage and around his arm to hold the bandage in place. "And this situation—"

"It's just as serious, I know." Jeshua winced. "Hebron in Judah is my best bet. It's probably the closest refuge city on this side of the Jordan River. Anyway, Hebron will do."

"If you think so."

"Think. Think," Jeshua said irritably. "I'm not try-ing to think. Hurry up with that bandage. I can't sit here bleeding all day. We've got to get out of here soon if escape is going to be possible."

Addan tightened the linen strip that held the bandage in place and caused Jeshua to wince. "Sorry."

"Are you sure about that?"

"About what?"

"Sorry. Are you? Knowing me may have cost you your life."

Addan reached the end of the linen roll and held it taut. "I . . . I hope not."

"Hmm."

"What?" Addan split the end of the unrolled linen strip, then tied the knot over the bandage.

"You. You really don't like reality."

Addan watched his thumbs touch the tips of his sticky fingers. "Your blood on my fingertips seems real to me."

Jeshua shook his head. "Like I've told you already." He reached for the clean tunic that Addan had taken out of the chest for him earlier and got dressed. "Your Rabbi Jesus has not done you any service with his teachings."

"They are old teachings."

"In new clothes." Jeshua beamed. "Beware. I wear new clothing. All things that shine brightly do not always have a higher value. Take off the clothing or scrape off the paint and you may discover—"

"What. What?"

A sardonic grin replaced Jeshua's expansive smile. "The truth. That's what. And don't ask," he looked into Addan's wide eyes, "don't ask, what is the truth? To ask is to challenge. And that will finish you like it did your rabbi."

Jeshua's eyes darkened. Madness caressed him. "Your Jesus battled with Satan. With the Devil. With demons. With dark angels. He was tempted! He was in conflict with evil. With himself. And with others, whom he exorcised—as he exorcised himself with the words: '*You shall worship the Lord your God, and him only shall you serve.*' Does that remind you of something?"

Addan nodded his head like a dumb mule. "'*Hear, O Israel, the Lord your God is one Lord, and you shall serve the Lord your God with all your heart and soul and mind and strength.*' Rabbi Jesus spoke within God's framework—within our scriptures. He spoke through God, not through himself. At least, that's what I thought I heard and saw and understood."

"Rabbi Jesus. Rabbi Jesus. Rabbi—what are you, boy? A disciple? A follower? A sympathizer? What?"

"I . . . I don't know."

"Why not?"

"I'm . . . I'm . . . I'm only a boy."

"Don't hide behind your age."

Addan licked his upper lip. "I—"

"Who are you?"

"I'm . . . I'm my father's son."

"Oh, brother. A rabbi, and a father. You've learned nothing from me. Nothing. Now my death will account for nothing. I leave nothing behind." Jeshua leaned toward Addan and whispered for dramatic effect. "You have succumbed to my evil."

"I have not."

Jeshua stood up and pulled aside the front curtain that was draped behind the driver's bench. "You'll not be saved by angels." He peered through the crack of light and studied the marketplace. "Hmm. Normal activity. So far."

"I've been saved by the word of God."

"Which you have abandoned through me."

Addan's defiance dissipated as he bit the knuckles of his left forefinger in terror. "I won't let you tempt me any further."

Jeshua released the curtain. "It's too late. You can never be fully devout. You've tasted the sweetness of evil. You can never go back. You can never be pure again. Your rabbi hasn't saved you."

Addan gazed at one of the crystals that still hung from the top rib of the wagon's canopy as if he were looking for a sign. A miracle. "You're being cruel."

"I am being truthful: You have fallen from grace forever," said Jeshua. "Forever. And forever will be here sooner than you think if we don't get out of here."

Jeshua walked to the rear of the wagon, pulled the rear curtain aside, and stepped outside onto the stage-platform as if nothing happened. He took a deep breath as if he were greeting a new day.

CHAPTER 16

Dagger

Addan stepped out from behind the wagon's rear curtain and onto the platform as soon as he heard someone confront Jeshua.

The platform trembled under Addan's feet.

Jeshua was already preparing the wagon for the road.

The stage-platform trembled again when Jeshua pulled out one of its support posts. He turned toward the man, who had addressed him, prepared to use the post as a weapon. "They're not here."

"My brother was not happy about you."

"I can't help that."

"He said he was going to do something about you."

"There's no need to, now. I'm leaving. See?"

"You don't understand. My brother said he was going to do something about you."

"I heard you the first time."

"You don't know my elder brother?"

"I don't know a lot of people."

"I saw him sharpen his dagger."

"A man should keep a sharp edge."

The man frowned. He pulled on his thick black beard. "I don't like you."

"You probably don't like a lot of people."

"I need to do something."

"I said there's no need to, now. I'm leaving. See?" Jeshua lowered the support post below his waist and presented it as a harmless article rather than as a weapon.

The man was unimpressed. "Nothing is that easy. Besides, I believe my brother was angry about something else." He placed his right hand on the handle of a sheathed knife that hung from his leather belt.

Jeshua stepped toward the man in response to the threat. "I've had enough of your clan." He brandished the support post and transformed the object back into a weapon.

The man stood his ground. "You better know how to use that."

"Do I need to?"

The man peered past Addan and tried to look into the interior of the wagon through the partially opened curtain. "Not if you let me have a look inside your wagon." Addan stepped in front of the opening and obstructed the man's view. "Get out of my way."

"Did you hear that, boy? This man thinks we may have kidnapped his . . . his—"

"Brothers!"

"Ahh. Both his brothers, no less. Ha! Did you hear that, boy? Did you?"

Addan forced himself to chuckle; the response sounded dry and nervous.

"And what kind of ransom could I expect from a clan of firewood vendors? No. Excuse me." Jeshua's lighthearted sarcasm grew. "A clan of rich firewood vendors. Right?"

The man's frown lifted toward a reluctant smile. Jeshua's charm bewitched him. "Well."

"Right? What enormous wealth could I hope to gain from you? A purse of gold? Or silver. Perhaps a pouch full of jewels can be found under that pile of wood."

The man guffawed. "You mock me, sir." The man's smile was complete. "And rightfully so." He attempted to look past Addan again and catch a glimpse of the wagon's interior. "But if they do not show up soon, well—you'll hear from me again."

Jeshua appeared crestfallen. "You don't trust me, sir."

"I trust in the weapon that you are armed with."

Jeshua glanced at the support post as if he'd discovered it in his hands. "This? A weapon? Can't you see? We are breaking camp. We are leaving. We have been convinced that you have a rightful claim."

The man's smile dissolved even though he was still under the spell of Jeshua's natural charm. "I know I am not a bright man."

"On the contrary, sir. You can see for yourself." He turned to Addan. "Hitch up the mules, my boy."

Addan hesitated, afraid to step away from the partially opened curtain.

"Go on." Jeshua glanced at the curtain then winked his right eye at Addan. "Close it. Tend to the mules." Jeshua turned back to the firewood vendor. "These kids. You have to tell them everything more than once nowadays."

"Yes. I have a boy like that as well."

Addan pulled the rear curtain closed as Jeshua continued to distract the firewood vendor. Then he jumped off the platform, glad to have something to do to hide his nervousness.

The man remained suspicious. Yet, impotent. After a long hesitation, he shambled toward the western side of the firewood pile where he posted himself like a sentinel and watched their every move.

Jeshua acted casually despite the pain in his arm. Fortunately, the full-length sleeve of his tunic concealed his bandage.

Jeshua laid the support post on the ground and pulled the remaining tee-pegs from the front edge of the platform. Then he pulled out the support pegs and lowered the platform.

He leaned against the wagon and took a deep breath. He felt dizzy. His arm throbbed. He felt the firewood vendor's presence; the man was searching for weakness. Jeshua straightened himself.

He reached inside the wagon and dragged out the wicker basket in order to deposit the tee-pegs—an unconscious habit, and in so doing he accidentally dragged out the bloody dagger that had been lying on the wagon's bed in front of the basket. Jeshua's pain and dizziness and tremendous effort to appear composed were costing him his ordinarily acute attentiveness. He did not see the dagger fall out of the wagon. Loading the support posts into the wagon, raising and securing the stage-platform in haste, and having to split his attention with the watchful firewood vender—all—compounded the error of not seeing the dagger. He walked to the front of the wagon and looked up into the driver's bench where Addan was already perched.

"The mules are ready," Addan whispered nervously. "Are you all right?"

"I'm fine."

"You look pale."

"I'm fine." Jeshua reached for his injured arm and felt wetness. He climbed on board and sat down. "Is there any blood showing through my sleeve?"

Addan leaned forward and stole a glance. "Yes."

Jeshua unlashed the reins from the hitching post. "Here. Take the reins. Drive us out of here."

"Into the city?"

"Don't get stupid now. Out of the city. Through the gate. Hurry. But be careful. Careful. We can't seem to be running. Well?"

"Well what?"

"What are you waiting for?"

"Sorry." Addan flicked the reins and whistled at the mules.

The wagon pitched downward then traveled smoothly in an arc toward Damascus Gate. Halfway into the wide turn around, Addan saw the firewood vendor approach their campsite where he bent down and picked up something.

"What are you looking at?" Jeshua asked.

"Look. The firewood vendor. Look."

Jeshua saw the dagger in the man's hand. "Hmm. That's not good. Now we don't have as long a lead to escape as I had hoped."

"I'm sorry."

"It's my mistake, boy. My mistake. Give me the reins." Jeshua snatched the reins from Addan and flicked them vigorously to force the mules to pull harder.

The world looked different to Addan, suddenly. He neither saw the splendor of the marketplace nor felt the excitement of approaching Damascus Gate. Now, it was a dark gauntlet that they had to pass through to escape. Now, he was truly running for his life. Addan felt sick to his stomach.

They passed through Damascus Gate going as fast as the traffic would allow. Jeshua almost ran over a porter carrying a wide bundle of flax. He had to pull back on the mules. "Careful there, Haga. Easy, Beba. It's my fault. My fault."

They funneled through the short and congested tunnel inside the gate's superstructure, slowed to a crawl, then burst into daylight again. All was a blur of confused color and motion. Traffic came and went from all directions, in all directions. The countryside seemed larger and wider and more distant now that they were on the run.

Addan hadn't noticed that they had already crossed the short bridge when he leaned over his side of the wagon to look back at the gate's entrance. "Nobody is pursuing us yet."

"It'll take him a while to figure out what's happened and then additional time to decide what to do. He's not very bright."

"I hope he's not."

Jeshua flicked the reins. "Me, too. Even at that, it'll take a while for him to explain what he thinks has happened to his brothers to members of his clan. Then it will take a while to report us to one of Jerusalem's garrison-sergeants. Don't worry. Even then, it'll take a while to get a lazy, Second Quarter sergeant-of-the-guard interested—Herodian or Roman. Don't worry."

"You mean, don't worry like you—The Master of Secrets."

Jeshua threw a sheepish glance at Addan. "You're a smart one."

"I'm a scared one. Scared to death."

"I know. I know. So am I." Jeshua whistled. "Come on! Pull your weight, Beba. Don't let Haga do all the work." He flicked Beba's reins. "Come on, girl. I need you more than ever."

CHAPTER 17

Hebron

The day was overcast. The Roman road was so smooth that it allowed Jeshua's mule-drawn wagon to maintain the higher-than-normal speed that Jeshua was demanding from them.

Addan sat near the right edge of the driver's bench. He leaned past the canopy to see if there was anybody behind them.

"There was nobody chasing us a moment ago," said Jeshua.

Addan righted himself. "No harm in looking." He sat erect.

Jeshua nodded condescendingly without taking his eyes off the road.

Addan pursed his lips. He glanced stiffly toward a tiny distant village on an area of high ground to the west. The dwellings were so closely built and so meticulously joined together by both stone and mud-brick walls for protection that the village appeared to be a discarded fragment from a large fortified city.

Occasionally, they drove past an independent mud-brick dwelling that could not hide the inhabitants' vulnerability or their poverty. They lived as farmers scratching a bad livelihood from the ground, lived as outcasts in the countryside, lived without security, and lived in mortal danger of raids by desperate vagabonds, cold bandits, and heartless murderers.

Jeshua reduced the mules' pace to keep them from over-exhaustion. "We'll stop in a little while to let Beba and Haga catch their breath."

"They need water, too," said Addan.

"You know where it is."

"Yes, I'll take care of it."

"There are two buckets inside. Neither one of them likes to wait for the other to either drink or eat." Jeshua grinned. "I spoil them."

"Look," said Addan, "there's a caravan approaching up ahead."

"I know. And this is as good a time as any to get off this road. How far did you say we were from Hebron?"

"I didn't."

"No matter." Jeshua pulled the mules to a slow walk and steered them southeasterly. "I believe we'll pass through Bethlehem first."

"That's right. If we make it that far."

"Sure, we'll make it."

The wagon stalled momentarily as the right front wheel hit the rise of the road's curb. The mules hesitated at the sudden increase in their load caused by this obstacle; they pulled harder to compensate.

The wagon shuddered from side to side as each wheel leaped over the curb. Once all four wheels cleared, the wagon continued to pitch back and forth and tilt from side to side as its wheels encountered the ruts of the primitive dirt road that branched off the paved Roman road.

"This rough road seems to have been avoided by most travelers," said Addan.

"It'll do."

"Do you think the magistrates in Hebron will give you—us—asylum?"

"I'm not going to ask. I'm going to try and disappear into the city if I can. I don't want to stand trial if I don't have to."

"But it was self-defense."

"Sure, sure. I'm an entertainer. A magician. A sorcerer. Remember? I'm tolerated because the common folk believe firmly in the power of magic." Jeshua grunted. "There's no stopping sorcery or soothsaying. Both Gentiles and Jews love it. Besides, it's good business. Anyway, I'm already living on the edge of the Law. I'm tolerated, boy, only if I keep out of trouble. And now. Well. They'll show no mercy to a suspected pagan—a heathen, at least. No. It'll be the stoning pit for me outside the city once I'm convicted of murder."

"Maybe not."

"I don't plan to find out. I'm certainly not going to volunteer. Once in Hebron, we'll try to disappear. If we're caught. Well. I'll certainly plead innocent before we're—" he coughed, "we're sent back to Jerusalem in chains to be judged and executed."

Terror struck Addan. "You don't think they'd stone me, do you?"

"Nah. I wouldn't worry."

"You're saying that to keep me calm."

"That's not true."

"Oh, sure. You're such a man of truth."

"All right. If it'll make you feel better, as soon as we reach Bethlehem, we can separate if you like. I'll give you enough money for you to get back to Jerusalem."

"I can walk back."

"All right. Then money for food and water."

"You'd do that for me?"

"There's no use in both of us getting executed."

"But—"

"They'll be looking for me and for my wagon. Not a stray boy in the countryside. You'll be safe. You can disappear."

"Thank you, Jeshua."

"Don't thank me yet."

Addan peered inside the wagon. "What are we going to do with those bodies?"

"We're going to discard them soon. We should also get off this road somewhere—ahh. Here's a place." He steered the mules off the dirt road onto a rocky trail. The wagon pitched and tilted, shuddered and trembled more ferociously on the rougher ground. "Over there. We'll hide them in that thicket."

"That's awfully sparse."

"It's what we've got. We have to get rid of them if there's any hope of escape."

"You mean, we have to lighten our load."

"That would help. But more importantly, we can't chance entering Hebron, or Bethlehem for that matter, with them still in the wagon. That would be stupid."

"I see. Hmm." Addan bit his lower lip. "And when is it, Master of Secrets, that we have been smart?"

Jeshua grumbled. "Don't go there, my boy. Don't go there."

The inadequacy of the thicket became more evident to Addan as they approached the patch of shrubs and underbrush. "There's thistle among those juniper bushes."

"Then be careful."

"Are we going to bury them?"

"Don't be silly. There's no time for that."

The right front end of the wagon tipped downward so steeply and so suddenly that Addan was almost tossed off the driver's bench.

"Hold on. Some of these ruts can be really deep."

"To ride on a wagon is a rare thing for me."

"I understand."

"How would you understand that?"

"Because I come from a tradesman family, like you. Not poor. But certainly not rich. Most of all, not exciting. Only the dull, day-to-day of existence."

"It's better than being alone. Or hungry."

"Bah. I like myself. And my wits have always kept my belly full."

"I see. And from which trade do you come?"

"I left the fullers trade and all that went with it—including my father."

Addan squirmed uneasily on the wagon's bench. "I see."

"What?"

Addan wrinkled his nose. "The fullers."

"I know. It stinks. I never got use to the foul odor of the cleaning compounds and bleaches. I hated having to tread on garments steeped in knee-deep water containing that noxious alkaline mixture. I hated it."

"I'd take pottery any day."

"So would I—growing up, that is. Wouldn't touch any trade like that now. Wouldn't do anything except what I'm doing."

"Which is?"

"Living, boy. Staying ahead of the world. Walking on the edge. But most of all, staying away from fullers that surround all towns and villages. Staying away from the constant chores of draining and filling vats with water, of cleaning and feeding the ovens below the vats with wood for the fires, of hanging new clothes and old garments up to dry."

Addan listened with adolescent enthusiasm; he was infected by Jeshua's rebelliousness.

Jeshua was amused by Addan's growing fascination. "In fact, my boy, even—whoa, Beba! Whoa, Haga." He peered in all four directions to see if they were being watched. "This will have to do."

"Their bodies will be discovered."

"Of course, they will." Jeshua winced as he climbed down from the wagon. "There's nothing we can do about that. Come on. We can't sit here all day."

"Is your arm all right?"

"Never mind my arm," Jeshua said irritably. "We'll see to it later."

Addan climbed down as well and followed Jeshua to the rear of the wagon. He unlatched the right side of the rear platform as Jeshua unlatched the left side; together, they lowered the platform. Once down, the edge of the platform almost touched the ground.

Jeshua reached into the wagon, pulled out the box that was used for stepping onto the stage-platform when it was erected, and set it on the ground near the wagon's rear opening. "Get in the wagon."

"Me?"

"Go on. You have two good arms. Drag out the closest one. Go on. I'll help you from out here."

"But—"

"Go on! There's no time."

Addan reluctantly stepped onto the box, pulled open the rear curtain, and peered into the wagon.

One man was lying face down. The other was on his back next to him.

Addan climbed into the wagon and grabbed the back collar of the man who was lying face down. Then he dragged him to the rear edge of the wagon and released him. "I've picked the leader of the firewood vendors first."

"Whatever." Jeshua reached into the wagon and grabbed the man's tunic by its collar. He frowned. "Do I have to tell you everything, boy? Climb out of there and help me drag him out."

"Sorry." Addan jumped out of the wagon without using the box-step and reached into the wagon for the dead man.

Together, they pulled him out and let him drop to the ground.

Jeshua noticed Addan's long and dark stare. "What now?"

"I can't believe I'm doing this. I can't believe this is happening to me."

"You believe too much. Grab the left shoulder of his tunic." Jeshua peered in all directions, once again. "So far, we're lucky. Not a traveler in sight." He grabbed the right shoulder of the dead man's tunic. "Over there. Among those junipers. Be careful. There are thistles among them."

They dragged the man into the thicket that was dominated by junipers, but was also fraught with thistles and weeds and nettles.

Addan bumped his left calf against one of the nettle branches. "Oww!"

"What did you expect?" Jeshua said crossly. "I told you to be careful!"

"Sorry." Several red streaks appeared across Addan's calf. He released the dead man's shoulder and swiped off the blood on his calf. "I was watching out for the thistles, but a nettle scratched me instead."

"That's what often happens in life. You guard from trouble in one direction, but trouble still comes from another. Get used to unexpected scratches. Come on. Let's get the other body."

In similar fashion, they dumped the second man beside the first then returned to the wagon.

Jeshua leaned against the wagon and frowned when he caught Addan shaking his head again. "Have a look at this injured arm of mine."

"I still can't—"

"Believe, already. Believe if you must!"

Addan nodded at Jeshua behind an unsteady calmness. "Right." He approached Jeshua and raised his wide sleeve above the bandage. "Your blood has soaked through."

"Wrap another dressing on top," said Jeshua. "Hurry. We shouldn't stay anywhere long." Addan climbed into the wagon. "Wait. Fill the two buckets with some water first and pass them out to me."

Jeshua brought the water buckets to the mules one at a time using his uninjured arm while Addan found a small piece of cloth to serve as a bandage and another linen roll of about three fingers width.

After Addan tended to Jeshua's wound, they threw the empty buckets into the wagon, raised and secured the platform, then climbed on board. They sat quietly for a moment on the driver's bench: Jeshua caught his breath and Addan calmed himself.

Jeshua untied the reins from the wagon's hitching post. "Here. Take the reins, Addan. You know the direction. Keep a careful eye on the trail."

Addan gently flicked the reins. The wagon eased forward, tipped to the left immediately, then righted itself. Addan knew how to get to Bethlehem and, at that moment, that's about all he knew.

CHAPTER 18

Guards

They had progressed steadily across the country-side without incident, without encountering a single pilgrim or merchant or vagrant. Addan had given up the reins long ago due to Jeshua's impatience with the boy's more careful driving. With the reins in Jeshua's hands, the ride was bumpier and wilder and, at times, dangerous. His right arm compensated for the injury to his left.

Addan held on with both hands: his right held onto the forward canopy's rib and his left held onto the front edge of the driver's bench. He leaned to his right and over the edge of the bench, as he had done numerous times, in order to see past the canopy behind him. He blinked his eyes carefully then blinked with terror. "Oh, my God."

"What?"

"There are six riders approaching us from behind."

"Six?"

There were several swatches of red and brown in the distance. "Yes." Addan leaned out further over the side to study the riders. "Four red cloaks."

"That's the Roman garrison guard."

"And two brown."

"You can be sure those are Herodian guards."

"Yes. Yes." Addan squinted hard. "I believe you're right. God! What are we going to do?"

"Keep running." Jeshua shouted at the mules, but there was no appreciable increase in their speed. "We're in for it now, boy!" He reached underneath the driver's bench and grabbed a whip with his left hand. "Sorry, girls! I'm going to have to use this!" He cracked the whip above them instead of striking them on their rumps. Their pace increased. Ignoring the pain in his arm, he cracked the whip above them again to make sure they would maintain full speed. "Good girls! Yeaah!"

Addan held on for life as he continued to study the garrison guards' approach.

The guards rode their horses hard and skillfully with their feet turned inwardly against their horses' bellies and with their torsos perched lightly upon their saddles. They appeared to be so balanced upon their steeds that it did not seem likely that any of them would fall off no matter how recklessly they rode.

As the riders shortened the distance between them and the wagon, Addan occupied himself by studying the details of their dress in order to stay calm.

The Roman and Herodian guards were lightly armored and without shields. They were all armed with long and short swords. Four of the six were each carrying a pilum-spear, the fifth was an archer, and the sixth—the one in front—was the sergeant-in-charge.

Their bronze helmets had short neck-guards with a pair of long and wide cheek-guards that flapped from their hinges. None of the helmets were fitted with a horsehair cresting, which probably indicated that they were a squad attached to a guard unit of a low status within the legionnaires of the region.

"How close are we to Bethlehem!?" Jeshua shouted.

"I don't know." Addan could not take his eyes off their pursuers. "I'm surprised that there aren't any kinsmen riding with these guards. I guess they probably don't own any horses."

"Ha! Good observation, Addan. A firewood vendor is not a rich living."   .

The left side of the wagon leaped off the ground when the front wheel hit a large rock.

"It brings food to the table," said Addan, in an attempt to remain calm, even nonchalant, at Jeshua's side.

"But not horses. Ha! And that's lucky for us in this case."

Jeshua seemed to be ecstatic by their predicament.

Addan tightened his hold on the wagon's forward rib. "Why?"

Jeshua cracked the whip. "Go, girls!" He cracked the whip again. "Because there won't be a brother or a cousin among them who will be unreasonable."

Addan squinted hard at the fast-approaching riders. "They don't appear reasonable to me. They look like they intend to kill us."

"Don't worry. They'll take us prisoner. That is, if we don't escape first!"

"I don't think that will happen."

"My girls have a lot left in them, boy!"

"Look whose avoiding reality now!"

"Ha!" Jeshua cracked the whip. The wagon fish-tailed on a patch of mud. "You're a quick study, boy!"

"I'm just seeing what I'm seeing."

"At least I won't have to maneuver into killing a kinsman and risk sure death with those guards."

"I don't understand."

"There's no stopping the hot temper of a blood feud. But those garrison guards behind us are getting paid for their living. They don't have anything personal against me."

"I hope not."

Jeshua whipped the mules. "Me, too."

"They're gaining on us, fast!"

"I know!"

The front left wheel of the wagon hit a wide and deep rut that almost tipped over the wagon. Addan was thrown backward into the wagon and Jeshua lost control of the reins as he grabbed a hold of the driver's bench and hitching post to prevent himself from being thrown out of the wagon.

"Are you all right, boy?"

Addan leaned out over the rear of the driver's bench. "I'm all right."

The mules kept running wildly.

"There's a pair of swords in one of the chests. Find them!"

"I don't know how to use a sword."

"They're not for you! I'll need both of them."

"You can use both?"

"I'll have to. I'll need to. Wounded arm or not."

Addan disappeared inside the wagon.

Jeshua heard the clamor of Addan's search within the tremendous jostling of the wagon. "Don't cut yourself, boy. Let the guards do that." Jeshua leaned perilously downward behind the mules and managed to grab hold of the dragging reins.

Addan leaned out over the driver's bench from within the wagon again. "Very funny."

Jeshua sat up with both reins in his control and released a crazy yelp that startled Addan and caused him to respond with a boyish giggle.

The dark laughter between them was all that was left of their morale.

The mules kept running hard without the whip.

CHAPTER 19

Swords

The mules grew tired, and the decrease of light that brought twilight did not come soon enough. When it did, dusk's glow lingered too long before the full onset of night could be used for concealment against their enemy.

"Easy, girls. I know you have nothing left in you." Jeshua pulled on the reins to stop the wagon and tied the reins around the hitching post. He stood up and noted the determination of the approaching riders before he climbed over the driver's bench and into the wagon. He snatched both swords from Addan.

The garrison guards surrounded the wagon. Their horses snorted heavily.

"Come out of the wagon!" The sergeant-in-charge ordered. "Don't make us come in after you!"

Addan trembled as he watched Jeshua unsheathe both long swords and handle them skillfully as if he knew how to use them. "What are we going to do?"

"We aren't going to do anything. You're no use to me now." Jeshua inhaled deeply, held his breath momentarily, then exhaled resolutely. "I'm going out there to either fight my way out of here or meet my end."

"This is the last time I'm going to order you to come out of that wagon!" said the sergeant-in-charge.

Jeshua slapped Addan's shoulder with the flat of one of his swords. "I'll see you in Gehenna, boy." He climbed out through the front of the wagon and onto the driver's bench, then jumped off like a madman and attacked the mounted guards.

The horses reared and neighed and trotted in small circles nearly out of control.

The sergeant-in-charge and the archer had their swords unsheathed; the other four men had their pilum-spears extended in the thrust position ready to either attack their enemy or to defend themselves. Each man also had a bludgeon strapped to the side of his saddle, ready to be employed in hand-to-hand combat.

The sergeant rode his horse toward Jeshua and swung his sword downward. Jeshua parried the considerable force of the sergeant's downward cut with the opposing edge of his own powerful sword. Then Jeshua countered with a thrust that forced the sergeant to strike Jeshua's sword aside with a sideways cut while he pulled his reins hard to back away his skittish horse with the other hand.

The archer attacked Jeshua, as the sergeant retreated, and threatened his opponent with a sideways cut toward Jeshua's hurt arm. Jeshua turned and positioned his sword across his body to deflect the attacking blade, then swung his other sword at the archer and hit him on the left cheek-guard of his helmet. This blow surprised the archer and made him almost lose control of his horse, which spun around twice. He pulled hard on the reins to keep his horse from going into a full gallop.

Jeshua heard another rider approach him from behind. He turned to meet his assailant: one of the two Herodian guards who was assaulting him with a pilum. Jeshua countered with an aggressive two-step attack that frightened the horse and prevented the guard from riding close enough to employ his pilum in an offensive thrust. Instead, the guard was forced to extend his pilum in defense. With the pilum fully extended, its wooden length was left vulnerable to Jeshua's powerful and lucky cut that broke off the front portion of the pilum, leaving a splintered end without a steel point, wavering helplessly at its target. Even though the splintered end still posed a considerable threat, the rider spun around on his horse to get away from Jeshua, who yelled like a man possessed by a demon. The madness and the frenzy of Jeshua's aggressive and continuous attack surprised the garrison guard.

"This man is deranged!" one of them shouted.

"No! He's gone berserk!"

"Possessed!"

"No! Crazed like a warrior should be!"

Ironically, these compliments diverted Jeshua from some of his cutting edge. His weakness as an entertainer was his need for applause, for verbal approval by his audience, for shouts of appreciation and respect by any opponent. Praise such as this reminded him of himself and, therefore, reminded him of the pain in his left arm and his overall fatigue. Although he continued to display a considerable amount of skill in his swordsmanship, in the end he could not recover his ferocity in the wake of his momentary lapse of self-awareness. He was finally surrounded by these men of superior fighting skill.

He grew weary of wielding two swords against the powerful and skillful cuts and thrusts of too many opponents. He was forced to discontinue his offense and concentrate all his attention on defense. Eventually, one of the Roman guards managed to maneuver his horse behind Jeshua and strike him on the back of the head with his bludgeon.

The impact of the blow stopped Jeshua from completing his next move. He was stunned into one position for a single moment before one sword dropped from his hand in mid-thrust and the other simply fell to the ground with him in mid-parry.

The sergeant brought his horse near Jeshua and looked down. "Nice one, Portius. You may have killed him."

"I don't think so, Sergeant Flaccus. He's a tough one."

"He's been on a battlefield, I think."

"He certainly fights like a warrior."

"Check him out."

Portius climbed off his horse and knelt beside Jeshua. "He's still breathing."

"All right. Tie his hands." The sergeant spun his nervous horse around to calm the creature then issued his next order to his two Herodian guards under his command. "Jidlaph. Heber. Check the wagon. There's a boy reported to be with him. Careful, now. He's probably as dangerous as this one."

"Right." Heber rode to the rear of the wagon, released the latches that held up the platform, and let the platform drop open. He stuck his pilum into the ground and unsheathed one of his daggers before he jumped into the rear of the wagon from his horse. He pushed the curtain aside and stepped inside.

Cestius, a Roman guard, came alongside Heber's horse and grabbed its loose reins.

Addan appeared in the front of the wagon and climbed onto the driver's bench. Then he jumped out of the wagon and lost his cap when he fell head-long on the ground. He rose to his feet and searched for the right direction in which to run.

Heber appeared from within the wagon and leaned against the back of the driver's bench. "Come back here, you little runt!"

The other men laughed.

"Is he too much for you?" Cestius shouted.

"Bite my rear end," said Heber. "Too bad that big, crazy one didn't cut your face in two. It took Portius to save your behind once again."

"Listen to him," said Jidlaph.

"And listen to you!" Heber was not amused. "Look at your splintered pilum. It seems to me you were also in defense—"

"Against a man, not a boy!"

The others continued to laugh.

Heber waved at Jidlaph dismissively and disappeared inside the wagon.

Addan looked in several directions to escape.

"Don't think about running, boy," said the sergeant. "Jidlaph!"

"Sergeant!"

"Bind his hands."

Jidlaph dismounted from his horse, handed the reins to the nearest rider, and grabbed Addan by the shoulder of his tunic. "Come here." He pulled Addan toward Cestius, the guard who held his horse. "This one is too frightened to speak. Hand me your rope, Cestius."

Heber jumped out of the rear of the wagon carrying a full wineskin. "Look at this! Our campfire will be easy to sit by tonight."

Jidlaph shook Addan. "Who is that man, boy? Speak up!"

"I . . . I don't know."

"Don't tell me that!"

"It's the truth. I've . . . I've only known him a couple of days. His name is Jeshua."

"We already know that."

"Leave the boy alone," said Cestius. "It doesn't matter what he knows." He tossed Jidlaph a short length of rope.

Jidlaph caught the rope with his free hand.

The sergeant-in-charge rode up to Addan as Jidlaph tied his hands behind his back. "Stay calm, boy, and we won't hurt you. All right?"

Addan nodded.

"Your name, boy."

"Addan."

The sergeant nodded. "Well, Addan, your master is a fine warrior." He spun his horse around one turn as he addressed his men. "Worthy of the battle, right men?"

The men cheered and agreed wholeheartedly.

"Great spirit!"

"Very capable!"

"A leader in battle."

"A fine maniac to have on one's side!"

The sergeant calmed his horse. "Portius. Cestius."

"Sergeant."

"Drag this Jeshua to the wagon and revive him. Use water if you must."

"There's water in the wagon," said Heber. He finally laid the wineskin against the rear wheel then climbed back inside the wagon.

Portius dismounted and handed his reins to Gessius. "I've got it." He unsheathed his short sword with his right hand and knelt beside Jeshua. He placed the palm of his left hand on his chest.

"Careful," said Cestius.

"Like I said, he's still breathing." Portius noted the blood on Jeshua's left arm. "He's been wounded." He raised the left sleeve of Jeshua's tunic. "But not by us."

Sergeant Flaccus dismounted from his horse. "That's the mark left by one of the murdered men. There was blood on the dagger found by the complainant."

"Then it wasn't murder."

"That's not for us to decide." The sergeant tied his reins around the wagon's hitching post. "Bring him over here."

Portius grabbed the back of Jeshua's collar and dragged him to the wagon.

"Where's that water, Heber?" the sergeant demanded.

"I've got it," said Heber, from within the wagon.

"I know there's probably another wineskin in there," said the sergeant. "Put a stopper on it! I don't want you drunk yet!"

Heber jumped out of the back of the wagon with a waterskin. "Sorry about that, sergeant. I couldn't help myself. It's mighty good wine."

"Give me that." The sergeant grabbed the waterskin from Heber. "Hobble those mules before they're spooked."

"Right."

The sergeant turned to Addan. "Where are the hobbles, boy?"

"Underneath the driver's bench."

Heber went to the front of the wagon to tend to the mules after hearing Addan's response.

Cestius led Heber's and Jidlaph's horses, and Gessius led Portius' horse as they rode their mounts to the wagon, dismounted, and tied all five horses to the wagon.

With Addan's hands tied behind him, Jidlaph brought him to the wagon. "Sit down, boy."

Addan sat near Jeshua's feet. Jidlaph stood close by and kept a watchful eye on him.

Sergeant Flaccus pulled the stopper from the waterskin. "Gessius."

"Sergeant."

"Start a fire. Darkness is almost upon us."

"Right."

"Cestius."

"Sergeant?"

"Picket the horses."

"Right."

"Let's see what we have here." The sergeant poured water on Jeshua's face and shocked him into consciousness.

Jeshua coughed. Rolled from side to side. Then tried to sit up. His injured arm and his tied hands against his back prevented him from doing so.

The sergeant reached down and helped Jeshua to sit up against the rear wagon wheel. "You gave us a good fight, there."

Jeshua continued to cough. "But not good enough."

The men laughed approvingly.

"He's one of us," said Portius.

"Never mind that," said Sergeant Flaccus. He scrutinized Jeshua. "You're in serious trouble, you know."

"Ha. I'm supposed to be the entertainer," said Jeshua.

Addan turned his head aside and stared at the ground where Jidlaph was standing. His gaze wandered toward the guard's large feet. They were dressed in heavily constructed sandals. He studied the guard's left foot. It had numerous belts attached to the thick sole and numerous belts wrapped around the ankle that were attached to a heavy strip of leather that rose up along the Achilles heel.

"I did not murder those men," said Jeshua. "I did not willfully, and with premeditation, take their lives."

"Yes. Well. Even if it was self-defense," said the sergeant, "there are four accusers who swear to your guilt."

"But the boy was there."

Sergeant Flaccus considered the boy then dismissed him emphatically by shaking his head. "The boy does not count."

"They are lying."

"They are citizens of Jerusalem. You are not. And the deceased are—or were—citizens, as well. Yes. We found the bodies."

Jeshua released a long exhale. "I see. So, there it is."

"It's no skin off my nose one way or the other," said the sergeant. "In fact, as far as I'm concerned, you're a better man than the two you left behind in that thicket."

"But?"

"But." The sergeant sucked on his teeth momentarily. "But they are respectable firewood vendors. And as I said, citizens of Jerusalem. And you. You are not respectable. You're a sorcerer and a nomad. A magician. A seller of potions and elixirs and dreams."

"Who told you that?"

"The firewood vendors who reported your crime against them also reported your reputation."

"I'm an entertainer. There's nothing wrong with—"

"That's not my concern. You skirt the Law by definition. And, therefore, you're already guilty."

"But I'm innocent."

"Not according to your accusers. And now, not according to the evidence."

"Besides," Jidlaph interjected, "God commanded his people to keep themselves away from pagan religious practices like magic or sorcery or divination."

"You see what I mean?" said the Roman sergeant. "You don't stand a chance. He's one of your people."

"He's nobody of mine," Jeshua declared.

The Romans among them laughed.

Jeshua sat up higher and looked at Sergeant Flaccus with pleading eyes. "But look—"

"I told you," said the sergeant. "You don't have to convince me. I understand that wound to your arm. And I saw your warrior courage. A man learns a lot from another man when in combat. You're no murderer. But I am not your judge. Sorry."

"You can still let us go," Addan interjected.

Jidlaph slapped the boy lightly on the back of the head. "Shut up, boy."

"Let the boy talk if he has the courage to," said Sergeant Flaccus. He addressed Addan. "And risk someone finding out? No, no, no. There are too many of us here. Wine will eventually loosen one of the tongues among us. When that happens, one or all of us may be arrested and even executed in your places. Sorry."

Addan was startled. "Your? You mean—me, as well?"

"What did you think was going to happen?" said the sergeant. "You're going back to face the same trial, my boy."

"I'm innocent!" Addan tried to stand up.

Jidlaph placed a heavy hand on his shoulder. "Where do you think you were going?"

"But I haven't done anything! I swear!"

"Give it up," said Jeshua. "They're not listening. They can't. There's no escape from laws centered upon 'if and then.'"

"Ho," said Heber, as he approached the cluster of men after having hobbled and cared for the mules. "We also have a scribe among us."

"I know a thing or two about the Law," said Jeshua. "And I know that the use of 'if and then' is no guarantee of resolving the question of my being right and their being wrong."

Heber laughed again. "If you want perfection, you are in serious trouble."

"He already knows that," said the sergeant.

Jeshua grimaced at Heber. "Facing any of our laws in court is a serious matter because of its flaws and imperfections."

"If a man strikes another man," said Heber, "and the man dies under his hand, then he shall be punished."

"Look who's being a scribe now," said Jeshua.

Cestius shouted from where he was tending to the horses. "I thought I was getting a headache from the blow to my head earlier. Now I realize that it's my head spinning from too much Jewish logic."

The Romans laughed. The Herodians did not.

"I was defending myself," said Jeshua, with exasperation.

"Prove it," said Heber.

"I have the boy there."

"Against what? The death of two men and the accusing word of those of their clan?"

"Besides," added Jidlaph, "this little one here also stands accused." He looked down at Addan. "It's into the stoning pit outside the city for you as well."

Addan bit his lower lip, too terrified by the possibility of the stoning pit to speak.

"The Law," Jeshua said contemptuously.

"And as Sergeant Flaccus already said," Heber added, "combine the accusation of legitimate citizens with the fact of your profession as a magician-entertainer who sells potions of questionable value, and, well—the judges will neither be understanding nor lenient with you. Their lack of sympathy will quickly lead to a sentence of death."

"I've seen your kind in my crowd before," Jeshua said contemptuously.

"I don't count," said Heber. "I'm common. But a court of law is not comprised of the common."

"I'll not be stoned," Jeshua uttered with great determination. "I did not murder those men."

The sergeant nudged Jeshua's left thigh with his foot, then crouched down beside him. "Come on. You've murdered somebody in the past. Come on, we're all guilty. Often, we're not caught. And when we are, even if we're innocent on that specific crime, we have escaped with plenty of other crimes that we have not paid for. Just think of it as payment—long overdue. The fact is, you did kill them—you can't deny that—and so . . . so, the leap to murder, in your case, as I see it, is not great." The sergeant shrugged his shoulders. "Innocent or not, I believe you're doomed."

"I know," said Jeshua. He glanced at Addan. "I know."

The glow of a fire emerged behind them.

"Ahh. It appears Gessius has built us a fire. Try to relax and enjoy this night's camp. You're among those who understand you. Some of us even sympathize with you." The sergeant shrugged his shoulders. "Rest. Wine. A meal. It's all we can give you." The sergeant's eyes hardened. "Don't make me lose my temper. Don't try to escape. I will kill you and the boy if I have to and take your heads back as proof of justice."

Jeshua nodded. "Justice. Yes." The darkness in his eyes deepened with his grin. "That campfire looks good. There's food and more good wine in the wagon."

The sergeant nodded with approval. "Good. Very good."

CHAPTER 20

Charm

The absence of moonlight deepened the darkness of the starless night. The dampness of the countryside could still be felt after the intensity and violence of the recent storms. Throughout Nisan, these storms were often possible, though often unexpected, during the season's "latter rains."

The campfire brought warmth and dryness and light. Hard men huddled around it wrapped in their thick red or brown cloaks. Their helmets and their unbuckled weapon belts were strewn by their sides. All of them were feeling full and drowsy from the food and wine that came from Jeshua's wagon. All of them were tired from the hard day's ride: from flight, in the case of Jeshua and Addan; and from the chase, in the case of the six Jerusalem garrison guards. The Romans in particular were used to living off the land either by forcing their will on the peasant population or by accepting their hospitality as a bribe to discourage violence against them. In other words, looting from Jeshua's wagon was considered a norm by these men—perhaps, even a moral requirement.

Cestius was the first one to belch. "I can seriously say to you, Jeshua, that I was surprised by your blow to my cheek-guard. You almost ended my days."

"Sorry about that," said Jeshua.

"You left quite a bruise on his face," said Gessius.

Cestius patted his cheek. "Yeah. It hurts a lot, too."

"Where did you learn to handle a sword so well?" asked Sergeant Flaccus.

"Oh. Here and there."

"Hmm. You don't act like a bandit," said the sergeant.

"I'm not. A rogue perhaps, but not a bandit."

The men laughed. Addan smiled and listened and kept quiet.

Heber stood up and stretched. "Who wants more wine?" All the men grumbled and nodded. "Everybody. I thought so."

"There's another skin in the wagon," said Jeshua.

"I know." Heber sauntered to the rear of the wagon and climbed inside.

"You're all right, Jeshua, as far as I'm concerned," said Portius. "Too bad you've wasted your skills in this strange occupation of yours."

"You? A Roman questioning the value of entertainment?"

"Then . . . then wasting your skills in this part of the world."

Jeshua nodded. "You might have a good point there. I'm constantly in trouble with these difficult Pharisees. They often claim that what I do is vulgar and bawdy. Vulgar indeed. I'm an entertainer. My performances are clean."

"Sure they are," Jidlaph said, facetiously.

"What?" Jeshua grinned mischievously. "I don't understand why they're so set against humor—and a little vulgarity."

The men chuckled.

"Now we finally get the truth," said Portius.

"Now, now," said Jeshua, noting their increased humor. "But seriously, I've always had to keep a lookout at my audiences to see if there was a spy or an officer of the court watching me for what they might call transgressions. Idiots." The Romans sneered with agreement. The Herodians chuckled with embarrassment. "So, whenever I saw one of these dangerous fools—" Jeshua peered at Jidlaph and then at Heber, who approached them with more wine from the wagon—"of course, I mean no offense to my brethren here—"

"No offense taken," said Heber.

"But seriously," said Sergeant Flaccus, "since you are speaking seriously, why have you chosen to do what you do? You would have made a better legionnaire."

"How do you know?"

"I've fought you."

"True. But I don't take commands well."

"I see. That would be a fatal flaw as a legionnaire. So. This living of yours. What do your audiences want?"

"Why," Jeshua's eyes brightened. "They want miracles. Magic. But mostly miracles, in the case of illness and physical maladies."

"Ho. So, you're a healer, as well."

"Ahhh." The alluring tone of a salesman's pitch enlivened Jeshua's voice. "I like to think of myself as a seller of potions."

"A crook," Heber interjected jovially.

"You hurt my feelings, Heber."

"I don't believe that for a moment."

Jeshua's charm increased with his mischievous grin.

"You're an evil one," Jidlaph interjected.

"Me?"

"You could ask God to cure them."

"Here we go again," said Cestius. "You Judeans and your God."

Jeshua ignored Cestius. "Nah. Too simple for the poor. Too inexpensive for the rich. There's no value in that. Understand?"

"So, you don't think there's any value in prayer?" Heber declared.

"Well. It gets a lot of public endorsement. But inside one's self. Privately. There is always too much doubt and too little result for anyone to truly believe in this thing called prayer." Jeshua noted Addan's drawn face. "Don't look so shocked, my friend. I suppose you prefer a prophet, like your Jesus, to be a miracle-worker who can scare away spirits and demons."

"He wasn't my prophet," said Heber.

"No matter. The point is, whatever he was or whatever you considered him to be, he was a fine magician nonetheless."

"True."

"A great one even. Not like me. No. He was certainly not like me, who chants incantations and who mixes strange substances inside the privacy of his wagon. No. He was not like me, who sells his services for a price and who practices black magic—the blacker the better. Yes. I am an unsavory fellow." Jeshua grinned. "And you should be frightened."

The Roman guards were amused and chuckled loudly at the expense of the Herodians, who chose to remain in good humor.

"He really is one of us," said Gessius.

Portius nodded approvingly.

Addan was more than frightened. He felt a growing silence within him. He looked out into the dark beyond the outer darkness of their campfire light like a sightless man looking for his soul from within his own blindness. Jeshua's charm frightened him.

"Anyway," said Jeshua, "as I was saying. Whenever I saw one of those dangerous idiots, I had to soften the comedy and stress the religious and educational elements. In fact, I would then have to rely more on my music to get myself past them and still keep my audience until those fools became bored or satisfied with what I was doing—or not doing. Fortunately, I'm a good musician. And I can sing a tune or two. Once they had finally left to make their report, the mischief could come out of me. My audience loved it. People love racy stories and songs and suggestive pantomimes and dances. I can do it all. I can play a beautiful pipe as well."

"Play for us then," said Sergeant Flaccus.

"That's a great idea," said Cestius.

The other men agreed enthusiastically.

"Gentlemen. Gentlemen." Jeshua presented his bound hands. "Look at my predicament. First, they were tied behind me. Then you were kind enough to retie them in front so that I can eat and drink with you. But to play, well, I need my hands free." He looked at the Sergeant. "Flaccus? Can I be trusted? It's up to you."

"No funny business, now," said the sergeant.

"To play was your idea."

"True." He looked at Portius. "All right. Untie him." The sergeant unsheathed his short sword from his belt. "But I warn you, you try to escape and I'll cut you down."

"Where's the pipe?" Heber asked.

"It's in a pouch behind the front chest on the left side of the wagon's bed," said Jeshua.

"Show me." Heber handed the wineskin to Gessius. "My cup is over there. Pour me a full one."

Gessius stood up. "I'll fill everybody's cup to the brim."

Heber waited until Portius untied Jeshua's hands. "Come on. Show me."

Jeshua stood up. "Right this way."

Jeshua's invitation sounded a little too casual for Sergeant Flaccus. "Go with them, Portius."

"Right."

The guards escorted Jeshua to the rear of the wagon.

Heber peered inside the dark wagon. "Don't you have a lamp?"

"You got the other wineskin in the dark."

"I'd already seen it before nightfall."

Jeshua pointed into the wagon. "It's back in there, inside a chest."

Heber climbed inside, stumbled and crashed to the front of the wagon, and opened the chest. "Now what?"

"The pipe is inside a small pouch."

"Here it is. I found it." Heber stumbled back to the rear of the wagon and handed the pouch to Jeshua. "Is this it?"

"Yes."

Heber jumped out of the wagon and accompanied Jeshua and Portius back to the main camp.

Jeshua sat close to the light of the fire. Then he took the pipe out of the pouch and inspected the instrument, which consisted of two ivory pipes joined together, each with a single-reed mouthpiece. Each pipe had five finger holes—four in the front and one in the back for the thumb.

Jeshua licked the reeds then blew gently into both pipes. A short melody came out of one pipe while the other pipe produced a droning background. The pipes produced a light melancholy sound. He stopped momentarily. "Where's my cup?"

Jidlaph brought him his wine.

Jeshua drank deeply. They all did.

When he finally played in earnest, the music was more melodic than rhythmic, which was unusual for this region of Palestine. The beautiful sound he made with his intricate melody deepened the growing somber mood at their campfire. His music sprang from deep within himself. He sometimes trilled brightly then plunged more deeply into a plaintive wail.

"For an instrument, which usually expresses joy, you have found a penetrating way to express your sorrow—your laments," said the sergeant.

"He plays like a condemned man," said Portius. "What else can you expect from him?"

"Thank you." Jeshua played on.

With only a few notes, Jeshua was able to produce another strangely appealing and possessing tune. In fact, he somehow managed to elevate the sound of this simple shepherd's pipe toward heaven itself.

The men were enraptured. Charmed. Even the campfire itself seemed to burn more brightly. Addan almost felt that there might be some hope.

Jeshua had a haunting way about his music. He bewitched the camp. He ended his last tune softly then laid the pipe on his lap. The silence that followed was calm and easy and comfortable.

Jeshua was relaxed. In control. Empowered.

The guards had softened. Had become friendly. Almost human.

Jeshua's entertaining skills were truly disarming and he knew it. This was his world. A place between reality and dreams. A place where people became vulnerable to him. And despite the pain in his left arm or the heat of his growing fever, he was able to capture his captors' full attention. He loved the power of this. He loved it.

Cestius stood up and stretched. "I'll go check the horses and mules." Heber leaned toward the campfire and fed it some wood. Jidlaph simply stood up and yawned. Gessius finished the wine in his cup. Portius reached for the rope to retie Jeshua's hands.

"Whoa, Jidlaph!" Jeshua exclaimed in an attempt to evade being bound again. "Stand right where you are. Don't move." He stood up. "I believe I see something behind your ear."

Jidlaph remained where he stood. "What. What? Is it poisonous?"

"Don't move, I said."

All the men became alarmed and prepared to reach for a sword.

Jeshua approached the Herodian guard. "Be very still." He reached behind Jidlaph's right ear and, suddenly, a small clay vial appeared. "Look. Ahh! One of my potions."

Everyone exhaled with relief.

"I didn't steal that," said Jidlaph.

"You'd rob his teeth if he slept with his mouth open," Heber declared.

Everyone laughed and relaxed once again.

Jidlaph frowned sheepishly. "Where did you get that?"

"He's throwing a bit of magic around." Sergeant Flaccus was amused. "You're a real character, Jeshua."

Jidlaph snatched the clay vial from Jeshua's hand. "What is this?" He was suddenly struck by a notion. "Wait. Is this something stronger than your wine?"

"What do you think?"

"Ha!" Jidlaph pulled the wooden stopper, wrapped with a piece of black wool, from the neck of the vial and sniffed it. "Smells good."

"It is good."

Jidlaph tossed it down in one large gulp. "Ahh! Sweet. Good. Is there one behind my left ear?"

Jeshua approached Gessius. "No. Behind Gessius' left ear." A vial appeared in Jeshua's hand.

Gessius chuckled and quickly snatched the vial from Jeshua's hand. "I'll take that."

"You're not man enough for that drink," said Jidlaph.

"A Roman can do anything better." Gessius pulled off the stopper, tossed down the potion, and threw the clay vial into the fire.

Jeshua approached the sergeant. "And what about you, Flaccus?"

"No. Not me."

Jeshua reached behind Flaccus' ear. Another clay vial appeared.

"I've had enough to drink." Flaccus assessed his men. "And so have my men."

The men grumbled.

"Cestius."

"Sergeant."

"Since you've been tending to the horses, take the first watch."

"Right."

"The rest of you know the order of the watch. Portius."

"Sergeant."

"Bind Jeshua's hands."

"Sergeant, sergeant," Jeshua said plaintively. "You don't have to do that."

"You're all right, Jeshua. But not all right enough to take your place at the stoning pit. Bind his hands."

The gaze in both men's eyes hardened.

Jeshua quickly softened. "All right, Sergeant." He extended his hands toward Portius. "How can I complain? You've been good to me—and the boy. I won't forget that."

Portius pulled Jeshua's arms toward him and wrapped his wrists with a rope. "Sorry, Jeshua."

"That's why you're still not a sergeant," said Flaccus. "Bind him well and check the boy's hands. Then bind them both to that wagon wheel." He stretched and yawned. "I'm going to sleep well tonight." He nodded at Jeshua. "The wine was good."

Jeshua smiled with great charm. "My pleasure."

"Come on," said Portius, who escorted Jeshua and a reluctant Addan to the rear wagon wheel. "I'll bind you both low on the wheel so you can sleep."

"That's all right," said Jeshua. "I'd rather sit up this night. I'll snooze."

"Sure. All right." He allowed Jeshua to lean against the wheel and tied his bound hands to one of the spokes with another length of rope. He checked Addan's hands to make sure Jidlaph had done a proper job earlier.

Jidlaph growled. "You don't have to check behind me."

"Since when?" Then Portius tied Addan to the rear wheel as well.

Jidlaph would have normally argued with Portius, but he was much more tired than usual. He wrapped his cloak around himself and lay down near the camp's fire with the others. Gessius was already hard asleep.

There were light chest-armor and helmets and hard sandals, pilums and bludgeons, weapon belts of swords and daggers strewn about. Each man used his saddle for a headrest and his cloak for a bed and blanket. The night was going to feel short for the garrison guards, who would sleep well from the wine. However, the night was going to be long for Jeshua and Addan, who didn't know if it would be their last.

CHAPTER 21

Escape

Addan pretended to be asleep. He shivered underneath one of Jeshua's blankets that Portius was kind enough to lay over him for the night.

He peeked at Jeshua from deep within one of the dark folds of the blanket that he also had pulled over his head.

Jeshua's own blanket was draped over his shoulders like a cloak. He was upright and awake and deeply in thought.

Addan felt tears roll down his cheeks. He wanted to go home. He wanted to be safe again. He wanted to hear the reprimand in his father's voice and see the disappointment in his mother's eyes. He wanted to go home and be a better son. He wanted to talk to those who knew Jesus as he had. He wanted to—

"I know you're awake," Jeshua whispered.

Addan sat up. "How did you know?"

"You were crying, weren't you?"

"No, I wasn't."

"Shhh. Whisper."

"No, I wasn't."

"If you're going to lie, do it well."

"You mean, like you?"

"Don't be so judgmental."

Addan's blanket fell to his waist. "I swear. You're evil."

"Well." Jeshua grinned. "Evil must exist."

"It does?"

"Sure. If life on earth is to be a testing ground for our behavior before God. Right?"

"Then . . . then you do believe in the God of Abraham."

"I never said I didn't. I'm a son of God as well."

"But Jesus—"

"I'm not Jesus. But I am the one who's testing you."

"Hmmm." Addan did not want to know what he meant by that. "How did you get those vials?"

"I snatched them out of the wagon when I was escorted to get my pipe. The cloak of darkness is always my great assistant. In any case, neither Heber nor Portius is very quick."

"What are we going to do, Jeshua? I'm frightened."

"So am I, boy. So am I." Jeshua looked toward the camp's fire. "Portius is finally on watch."

"So?"

"He's the most sympathetic of the lot." Jeshua tried to reach into his tunic then winced.

"How is your wound?"

"It's burning. And I'm sick. And I don't have time for either of those conditions."

"What are you doing?"

"I'm trying to get at my dagger."

Addan became more alert. "Where did you get a dagger? They searched us carefully."

"Where I got the vials, my boy."

"Ahh. The cloak of darkness. I see."

"I wish I could have tricked a couple more of them into drinking them."

"I don't understand."

"Jidlaph and Gessius won't be waking up—"

"You've poisoned them?"

"Shhh. Calm yourself, boy. I've only drugged them. They're sleeping deeply, that's all." Jeshua shook his head. "Two more. All I needed was two more to have taken a vial and the odds would have gone to my favor."

"The sergeant is pretty smart."

"True. And he goes strictly by the rules—by Roman military rule. Well. At least, close enough. Look out. It's Portius. Pretend you're asleep. Quick."

Addan lay down and closed his eyes and Jeshua leaned against the wagon wheel and pretended to sleep. Portius approached and studied them for a few moments. He turned from them feeling satisfied that the prisoners were secured. Jeshua carefully opened his eyes and watched Portius go to the horses and mules to make sure they were still securely tethered and hobbled and content.

"He's gone," Jeshua whispered.

"What now?" murmured Addan.

"We're going to make a break for it."

Addan sat up again. "Escape? But Portius is on watch. He looks awfully lively to me."

"And, like I said, he's also the most sympathetic to me. Maybe. Just maybe—"

"Look who's dreaming now?"

"This is true life and death, boy. It's the only place where hopes and dreams have a place and, in fact, can actually do some good."

"If you say so. What are you doing?"

Jeshua was finally able to get a hold of the knife he had hidden in the breast of his tunic. "I'm going to cut myself free. Keep your eyes on Portius."

Addan sat up more erectly: alert and frightened and hopeful. "Are you going to cut me free, too?"

"No."

"Jeshua."

"Of course I am, you dolt. Your eyes. Keep them on Portius." With the dagger inverted in the palms of his tied hands, he was able to saw at the rope in short strokes. "I'm glad this blade is sharp. There." The rope was loosened enough with its first cut to allow him to unravel the rope and free his hands. "Where's Portius?"

"He's still with the horses."

"Good. Don't take your eyes off of him." Jeshua eased toward Addan and grabbed his bound hands.

"He's talking to the horses."

"That soft heart will cost him someday."

Addan kept silent and studied Jeshua as he cut through the rope and freed his hands. "A hard heart will cost a man as well."

"Yeah. Sure. Come on." Jeshua went around the rear of the wagon and waited for Addan. He pointed straight out into the outer dark. "You go that way. Easy does it. No fast moves. And if you hear Portius

221

sound the alarm, you keep running in that direction."

"But—"

"No buts." Jeshua crept toward the front of the wagon.

"Where are you going?"

"We're on our own from here on out."

Addan scurried toward him. "We're what?"

"Each man for himself, boy."

"I thought—"

"You think too much. Get away from me. I need a horse." Jeshua looked at his dagger, then at Addan. "I don't want your blood on this dagger anymore than I want to see Portius' blood on it. But so help me—"

Addan backed away from Jeshua. "You're no better than them. And you're no better than any of the murdering bandits that roam the countryside."

Jeshua's ugly snicker sounded like the low growl of a leopard just before a kill. "It's about time you figured that out."

Addan backed away further from Jeshua. He shook his head. "I see. All right. I'll stay here until you're on a horse."

"You don't owe me anything, Addan."

"It's not for you."

"Ahh. Repentance. You Jesus followers are insuf-ferable."

"You be what you are and I'll be—well, I'll be . . . be something else."

Jeshua snickered. "Whatever." He peered over the front of the wagon at the horse picket. "Where is he?" He crouched, eased around the front of the wagon, and approached the horses.

Addan leaned against the hidden side of the wagon feeling sick. He knew he'd stand a better chance to escape if he made a run for it now. There was a good chance in this darkness to gain some distance and find someplace to hide before day-break. Still—if they were able to find the dead bodies so easily, they could probably track him and run him down with their horses by mid-morning. Still—

Run. Save yourself. At least, try.

Addan was paralyzed. Physically. And emotion-ally. He bit his lower lip. He clenched his fist. He waited for Jeshua to escape. The cry was like the sudden sound of breaking glass.

"Escape! Escape!"

The sound of men rousing each other from their slumber and the sound of unsheathing swords followed almost instantly.

Addan's heart began to pound so hard that he thought it was going to leap out of his chest.

He pushed himself away from the wagon and ran into Heber, who was huge and hard and powerful. Heber gripped Addan's throat. His right upper arm was like a pair of carpenter's clamps.

"Hold still, boy, or I'll snap your head off."

Addan relaxed like a hooked fish that had hanged too long out of the water.

"Good," said Heber. He released Addan's throat to let the boy breathe, spun him around then grabbed him by the hair of his head and by his left upper arm. "Let's go." He pulled Addan toward the camp's fire where Jeshua was fighting for his life.

Addan watched helplessly. Hopelessly.

Jeshua's potions had been effective. Jidlaph and Gessius had been unable to rise to the alarm.

Jeshua had a bludgeon in one hand and his dagger in the other. Portius was sitting on the ground with his left hand on his head and his right arm extended behind him for support.

Jeshua had chosen to hit Portius instead of stab him.

Had this been a fatal mistake?

Addan shook his head. Probably not. Because if Portius saw the bludgeon, he would have also seen the dagger coming and would have managed to sound the alarm anyway.

Good for you, Jeshua. Good for you.

The horses and mules were nervous and frightened and tried to stay out of the men's way. Jeshua tried to get between two horses to shield himself from Cestius' and Flaccus' swords, which he had managed to parry clumsily with the bludgeon. His dagger also prevented his opponents from stepping in too closely; they knew Jeshua was familiar with combat and did not want to step within the fatal swing of his blade.

The horses and mules neighed and snorted and tugged at the picket line to break loose.

"I'll see you in Gehenna!" Jeshua cried. Then he laughed like a madman.

The moment of defeat was a sudden shock of surprise as Portius managed to rise then run him through with his long sword from behind.

Addan heard the sound of the broad steel blade cut through bone and muscle. Addan closed his eyes.

The sound of Portius pulling out the sword was almost as loud. It forced Addan to open his eyes again.

Jeshua dropped to his knees. Blood streamed suddenly from both corners of his mouth. His eyes became glassy. Then he fell, facedown, on the ground.

"See? That's what we get for being nice," said Sergeant Flaccus.

Portius shrugged his shoulders. "Can anyone here say they wouldn't have tried to do the same thing?"

"Your heart will cost you your life someday."

"You liked him as well."

"Yeah. Well. My mistake," said the sergeant. "Let him bleed out right there. We'll throw him into the wagon in the morning."

Heber brought Addan to Sergeant Flaccus and threw him on the ground next to Jeshua. "What about this little fish, sergeant?"

"What about him?"

"I say let's kill him."

Sergeant Flaccus grimaced as he studied the boy. "That might not be a bad idea. Cestius."

"Sergeant."

"See if you can roust Jidlaph and Gessius from their slumber."

"I don't think it's the wine that's kept them down."

"I know, I know. It was Jeshua's vials," said Sergeant Flaccus. He kicked Jeshua. "You clever rogue." Then he kicked Addan. "Are you clever too?"

Addan was too terrified to speak in his defense.

"I say kill him."

"Yeah. Kill the little runt."

Addan closed his eyes and prayed.

CHAPTER 22

Prayer

Where is my hat?

Where are my sandals?

Help me, my Lord.

Help me, my Lord.

If I keep my eyes closed, nothing will happen. If I don't listen, they will not harm me. If I keep silent, I will disappear.

Oh, God. I ache to go back to the beginning—to go back home, to trust my mother's love.

Please let me wake up. Please let this be a dream.

I won't strike a bargain with you: I've watched my father; and my mother. I know it doesn't work that way.

Can I ask for strength?

Am I worthy to understand your loving presence?

If so, what does this presence mean?—my Lord and my God .

What is this . . . this prayer that I am offering you?

Are you listening? Or am I speaking to myself?

I am—frightened.

I am—sorry.

I am—lost.

My Lord and God, I am guilty before you. Please grant me the strength to discover the true secret in my heart. Please make me more genuine so that my sorrow can arise from having offended you rather than having this—my sorrow—arise from the shame of being caught, or arise from the pain of a wounded love for my self.

Forgive me. Even if it's only for this—my final moment before you. As I am now.

I no longer feel cold.

CHAPTER 23

Men

"I say, kill him!"

Addan opened his eyes. Six angry men towered over him.

Jidlaph and Gessius were still groggy from the drug-induced sleep caused by the contents of Jeshua's clay vials. Heber was heatedly angry. Portius was countering that anger with his own. Cestius was cheering Heber on. Sergeant Flaccus stood stiffly, his cold eyes fixed upon what to do next.

"There's no point in killing this boy," said Portius.

"Since when does a Roman need a point to kill?" Heber countered.

"I don't think there's anything to lose in that," said Cestius. "Sergeant?"

"Who cares about this little fish," Portius interjected, before Sergeant Flaccus could respond.

"Portius is right," said Gessius. "Who cares?"

"I care," said Jidlaph.

"So do I!" said Heber.

"But we've caught our criminal," Gessius added. "We've brought him to justice. Behead Jeshua and leave his body for the wolves and hyenas and carrion birds."

"I don't know about that," said Jidlaph.

"That's a fine idea," said Cestius.

"Whoa, wait a minute," said Heber. "I don't know about that."

"What's there to know?" Cestius added. "Let's place his head on a pilum as proof of this justice upon our entering Damascus Gate. We can present it to the accusers and the court of judges. Sergeant?"

"That's a fine idea," said Portius, before Sergeant Flaccus could respond. "In so doing, there's no need to kill the boy. Nobody will care about the boy."

"I'll care about the boy," said Heber.

"Why?" asked Portius. "Because he's one of your kind?"

"I know how these little buggers operate," said Heber.

"Because you were just like him as a boy, is that it?"

"Bah! Look at him. There's too much woman in him for that to be true."

"Therefore, nobody will remember the boy," said Portius.

Heber softened when he looked at Jidlaph, who shrugged his shoulders. "Well. I suppose you're right."

"Of course, he's right," said Cestius. "But enough about the boy."

"That's right," Gessius interjected. "If you don't like the idea of leaving the body upon the ground, Jidlaph, then after we cut off his head and put it on the end of my pilum, we can leave the body hanging by its feet from the limb of that tree."

"It's still a defilement of the land that God has given our people," said Jidlaph.

"What people?"

"My people," Jidlaph said proudly.

"And those who live nearby," Heber added.

"And those who have to walk and ride past that tree," said Jidlaph.

"Good!" said Cestius. "Let the headless corpse hang and be a warning to these . . . these local inhabitants."

"I could be one of them," said Heber.

"You're a soldier. A garrison guard like the rest of us. That's where your allegiance lies."

"Cestius is right," said Gessius. "You Herodians are taking this too seriously. We leave crucified corpses on exhibition all the time. What's your problem?"

"That's true," said Portius, trying to encourage Sergeant Flaccus to state his opinion. "What are you two getting so upset about?"

"I can go along with defilement," said Jidlaph, before the sergeant could respond, "as ordered by my superiors." He nodded at Flaccus. "But I won't make a sport of it."

"Careful," said Sergeant Flaccus. "I see no sport in anything that's happened or whatever it is I will choose to do with this criminal. The simple fact is, he tried to escape. And in so doing, he forfeited whatever honor he had earned with us. Furthermore, if he had succeeded in escaping and we were forced to return with an empty wagon—you, along with the rest of us—might have had to pay for that loss with our lives."

"Or risk a terrible flogging at the very least," Portius added.

"I'll not be flogged," said Cestius.

"And I'll not agree to this defilement," said Heber.

"Be careful," said Sergeant Flaccus.

Heber released Addan and approached the sergeant. "I've never liked you from the beginning."

"And I don't like you. So what. You'll obey my orders or—"

"What?" Heber pushed Sergeant Flaccus.

Everybody brought their swords to the ready.

"Hold on," said Portius. "This is going too far—over what? What?"

"The truth has finally come to the surface between us." Heber glared. He stared hard at Sergeant Flaccus. "I'm glad."

"What truth?" said Flaccus. His sword threatened Heber in earnest. "Herodian swine. You're not worthy enough to be in the Roman guard."

"Swine?" Heber threatened Flaccus with his sword. "I'll show you how powerful my presence can be."

"You'd better be able to back up your words," said Portius.

Heber struck the first blow.

Sergeant Flaccus thwarted the attack effortlessly. "This is going to cost you." He swung his sword downward in earnest.

Heber parried successfully.

They fought. The others watched with an enthusiasm often seen at a cockfight.

Addan could not believe what he was seeing.

Was this going to be to the death or was this the ritual challenge of men and authority? Only the flow of blood or the lack of it would be the true answer.

The sound of steel. The shouts of men. The grunts of combat. The intensity of the fight, all—made Addan invisible again.

Addan shuffled away from them on his hands and knees. A single shuffle and a long pause at first. Then two and a pause. Three. And finally, a steady scurry into the night until the growing distance from them made him feel safe enough to rise and run for his life. He stumbled in the darkness. He rose again. Then he ran as if there were no life left.

As he traveled beyond the outer darkness, he thought he heard the sound of their swords come to a stop.

"Wait!" said Gessius. "The boy! He's gone."

Sergeant Flaccus and Heber pulled away from each other. They were breathing and sweating heavily.

Portius began to laugh.

Both men lowered their swords.

"Shall I run him down?" asked Gessius.

Sergeant Flaccus joined in Portius' laughter, which infected the other men. "No. Let the little fish run home to mother. He can tell her how he escaped the big bad garrison guards of Jerusalem."

Their laughter erased their anger and ended the fight. Heber sheathed his sword and offered an apology to the sergeant.

Flaccus waved him away as if nothing had happened. He cautiously approached Jeshua and slowly raised his sword in order to cut off Jeshua's head with one powerful stroke.

CHAPTER 24

Women

Addan ran and stumbled with an abandon that he never thought possible. He was like a wild animal, too afraid to be careful. He tripped often; he stumbled and fell numerous times—each time, he arose from his fall with a greater and more intense fear. After a while, however, he had run so hard and had run so long that even his terror could no longer sustain him. He finally stumbled and fell breathlessly to the ground unable to get up, unable to go any further.

He gasped and wheezed and rolled from side to side on the ground trying to catch his breath. His only comfort had been the concealment of the darkness, which was lifting toward dawn.

He no longer cared.

Let the light come.

He was resigned.

Let the end come quickly.

The light came. The end did not.

Addan sat up feeling weary and empty and alone.

He stood up and started walking without a destination. Not in a trance. Yet, not in his full mind.

His bare feet were sore and bleeding. His tunic was filthy but dry.

He stopped walking. He saw the back of a tiny mud dwelling.

Smoke arose in front of the very humble abode. He remained cautious as he approached.

He glanced behind himself—a habit caused by fear and terror. Now that daybreak was upon him, he was afraid that the garrison guards would appear on the horizon tracking him in order to run him down and take him captive again.

He kept a respectable distance from the dwelling as he eased around it in a wide arc toward the front of the windowless structure.

The roof was constructed of strong reeds long enough to support palm branches with dried leaves that were woven into the reeds in a patternless manner. The roof was more useful against the sun than it was against the rain.

The smoke came from a cooking fire that burned underneath a large metal cauldron with three long and thick metal legs projecting from its bottom, which held the cauldron upright, as well as provided the distance necessary for the wood-fire to burn freely.

Addan smelled onions and garlic and beans.

An old woman stooped over the boiling cauldron. She stirred the contents of the cauldron with a long piece of wood. She stirred with an attentiveness so deep that she looked like a penitent. She ignored him.

Her tattered, full-length outer garment was matted and threadbare, torn and moth-eaten; the fabric was so dark brown that it looked black. She wore a second full-length garment underneath, a tunic, which revealed itself at the collar. A third article of clothing underneath the tunic was also evident by observing the wrists, where the differing lengths of each garment's sleeves exposed all three layers. Together, these multiple layers of heavy fabric were so thick that the garment was as stiff as a suit of armor.

Her clothing made her appear big and heavy, but her hands were not. Thick white strands of hair peeped out from the front of her mantle. Her dark countenance appeared stern, but her eyes were not.

She glanced at Addan. She revealed more of herself with her silence.

The skin of her face was dark and rough and mapped with deep lines that were caused by her age, by the sun, and by the pain of long-suffering and sorrow and poverty. Her mouth formed a permanently rigid frown that refused to be apologetic. Her large, hawk-like nose intensified her perpetual scowl. The shock of her white eyebrows, which sprouted wildly across her brow, was a sharp contrast to her faded black mantle that framed her face and made her appear as if she were in mourning.

The old woman stared into her boiling cauldron of beans. "Are you a Galilean?"

Addan nodded.

"Speak up, boy. You have nothing to fear from me. I'm neither a Roman nor a man."

"Yes."

"What's a lost Galilean boy doing in Judea's countryside?"

"Looking . . . looking for my father."

"Ahh. And what's your father's business here?"

"He's . . . he's a disciple who came—"

"Ahh, yes, yes. Another follower. Which prophet is it this time? There are so many."

"The one called Jesus. Of Nazareth."

"Yes, yes," she mumbled, "of course, the Nazarene, recently crucified, the Nazarene, like you, the Nazarene, not surprising, the Nazarene . . ." her voice grew softer as she continued to repeat herself, " . . . the Nazarene," until her voice trailed off into an undecipherable whisper, " . . . Nazarene . . . azarene . . . arene . . . ." She stabbed at something in the cauldron with her stick. "And you?"

"Me? Me what?"

"Are you a disciple?"

"My father—"

"You! You, boy. What about you?"

"I . . . I've heard his words."

"Hmm." She stirred her beans. She stared into the steaming cauldron. "And you are questioning these words now."

"I . . . I still seek to understand them."

The old woman continued to stir her boiling beans. "Hmm. You have potential." She stopped stirring and straightened her broken body as well as she could. She studied Addan for a few moments. "Men always speak with great certainty when they address women." Her permanent frown deepened.

"You'll change as your youth disappears into man-hood."

Addan searched the horizon from the direction he had come. "I don't know how much more change I can take in my life."

She pulled the long cooking stick out of the cauldron and pointed the wet and steaming imple-ment at Addan. She used it to emphasize her words, but it appeared as if she were waving a wand to cast a magical spell on him. "Beware, beware, change is always in the air," the old woman chanted. She inhaled suddenly and checked whatever it was that she was about to say. "Beware." She plunged the lower end of the wooden stick into the boiling caul-dron and stirred. "The truth. Who are you running from?"

"The Law."

She cackled. "What Law is that?"

"Roman Law, I think. I fear."

"Yes. Cloaked in our Law." She sneered. "Widowed by Rome. Raped by Rome. Motherless by Rome. Disfigured and disgraced by Rome. Don't speak of Roman Law to me. Don't speak to me of God's Law, either."

Addan ran the fingers of his left hand up his forehead and was reminded that his cap was missing when his fingers ran through his hair as well. "Jesus said—"

"Nothing new, I'm sure. Go on. Keep your wisdom to yourself." She cocked her head to the right in an attempt to study him more carefully with her good eye. "Are you a thief?"

"I . . . I don't know."

"Hmm. You are too honest with yourself. That's good. But that can be fatal."

"I escaped from Jerusalem's garrison guard during the night."

"Then you're safe."

"I've been running from them for the better part of the night."

"And if they wanted you, they'd have run you down by now."

"You don't understand. I was involved in—"

"Say no more. I don't need to hear your confession. Your eyes tell all, my pretty one." She stirred the cauldron and chanted. "The darkness of our deeds is carried into the beyond, the darkness of our thoughts will torment us forever." She released the stick and left it in the cauldron. "Sit down by the fire. You look hungry."

"I'm . . . I'm not hungry."

The old woman cackled. "You don't know enough not to be hungry. Sit. Never refuse food. Eat. Then be gone."

CHAPTER 25

Dinah

The old woman had been right. Her food made him feel better. Her rough kindness had made it possible for him to go on. Somehow, he was less afraid. He was more uncertain than anything else. But clear minded. And now, with a purpose other than running from bandits or legionnaires or himself.

He had to go back to Golgotha. He had to stand at the place of the skull on his own two feet. On his own. To face whatever it was that he had to discover for himself. If anything.

"Oh, God. Please let there be anything. Anything at all that I can understand."

He walked steadily toward his destination without thinking until he finally approached Golgotha. Then a growing uncertainty began to agitate his mind.

He looked up at the three crosses from the foot of the mound.

Bleak.

The auxiliary garrison guards were indifferent to his presence.

He did not notice the woman lying on the ground.

Addan approached the crosses on the mound.

He did not understand what drew him back to this desolate place again to face the emptiness that Jesus left behind. But here he was nevertheless. Nevertheless.

Addan stepped toward Jesus' empty cross, knelt before it, and touched the wood of its stake.

Nothing. He felt nothing. Then he cried.

The sounds of his childish sobs awakened the large brutish thief who'd been crucified with Jesus. The man Addan knew to be Azriel. "What is this? Who are you? I don't know you!"

Addan turned and looked up at Azriel. "I was a follower."

"Oh, brother. Another one. What are you . . . you doing here? I'm . . . I'm the only one not dead yet. Ha! Come here, boy." Azriel writhed. "Pray to me if that'll make you happy. Ha! That's right. Pray to me!"

Dinah raised her head in response to Azriel's shouting. She did not rise. She chose to watch. She chose to be invisible.

Addan rose then leaned against Jesus' cross for support. He glanced at the auxiliary guards with concern. One was asleep. The other was sitting on the ground beside his comrade. Both were wrapped in their cloaks. Both continued to be disinterested in him. He looked up at Azriel again. "I . . . I—"

"Bah! Another lunatic!"

"I can pray for you."

Azriel laughed. "Come here, boy. Come closer."

Addan came closer.

"See that sponge floating in that bowl of wine there?"

"Yes."

"On the rod, boy. Raise it to me on that rod, boy."

Addan considered the request.

"Go on," said the auxiliary garrison guard who was awake. "All you'll do is keep him alive to suffer longer."

The other guard sat up from his half slumber. "Go on, slake the beast's thirst."

Both guards laughed.

"Hurry, boy," Azriel croaked. "Before they change their minds."

Dinah almost intervened by running to the bowl of posca-wine herself to bring comfort to her Azriel, but held back. She recognized the harsh game men often played with each other and realized that a woman's interference would dampen the pleasure of their cruel sport and cost Azriel his possible drop of comfort; she decided that it was best to remain invisible.

She watched and hoped that the boy was successful.

Addan went to the large bowl of posca, grabbed the nearby rod, and stuck one end of the rod into the wine-soaked sponge that he had lifted out of the bowl. Then he extended the rod upward to raise the sponge to Azriel's burnt and cracked mouth.

Azriel sucked on the vinegar-stinking, posca-soaked sponge like an animal sucking the blood of its freshly killed prey. Addan held the sponge in place until Azriel had drained all that the sponge had to offer.

When Addan retracted the rod to lower the sponge, Azriel suddenly rose above his misery and exhaustion. Approaching death, he reached for the last of his powerful strength, like a lamp's flame that suddenly brightens when reaching for the last of its precious oil just before it dies. "You will also perish in this lonely place. Like me. Like your Master Jesus. He had to face his own miserable end like anybody else. There's no escape. In the end, there is only pain and suffering and emptiness." He coughed up blood.

"But . . . but he was more—"

"What? You think that Galilean, that, that, Nazarene was more than human? You think he was the Messiah?" Azriel laughed, then winced. "And what if he was? What good would that be? What good has it done? What portion of the messiahship has he fulfilled? What? Where? Where is his kingship? Where is Rome? Where is the peace? Answer me, boy. Answer me!"

"His miracles proved—"

"Bah! Any prophet. Any sorcerer. Any healer. Any messenger can perform tricks." Azriel studied Addan's expression with what was left of his one good eye. "Those miracles—"

"Were for the good of the people."

"People, people," Azriel muttered breathlessly with contempt. "Bah! People are not worth dry spit! They care about nothing. Trust nobody! Believe in

251

nobody. It's all a dream, this thing called love and caring and—bah! People. They're mean and ugly. They're selfish and cruel. They'll kill you for the thinnest copper shekel."

"But Jesus said—"

"Jesus said. Jesus said." Azriel gasped for breath. "Save yourself, boy. Don't believe in anything." Azriel winced from his deep and miserable pain then somehow gathered enough breath to laugh. "Death is not to be feared because there is nothing after death." He writhed from the pain it caused to speak to Addan with so much conviction. "There's no God, you idiot. And there's no messiah. There's only suffering."

Addan trembled.

Azriel wheezed. "You've come close, boy. You think you've been walking in Satan's shadow." He bared his teeth. "There's no Satan, boy! Ha! But you think you've been apprenticed to Satan and you believe in a demented lunatic." He reached for his breath. "Get out, evil. Get away, death. Save yourself, boy, before it's too late. Save—your—" Azriel had neither the breath to continue to speak nor the strength to remain conscious. His head dropped forward in a comatose bow. The difficulty of his respiration and the intensity of his emotions left him in a restless unconsciousness.

Dinah, who had been standing by listening, approached the boy. "Who are you?"

She startled him. "I'm . . . I'm nobody."

Her sensuousness instantly aroused him. Addan was shocked and embarrassed by these feelings toward her, which she sensed and smelled and recognized immediately. She softened her contemptuous eyes in order to disarm Addan further with her feminine charms. She knew he did not understand his feelings. That he was an innocent about to be a man. An innocent who could neither take his eyes off her braided hair, nor take his eyes off the top of her exposed shoulder.

"No. No, you're not—nobody." She looked at her man Azriel. "Because those were the kindest words I have ever heard him speak."

Addan was surprised. "Kind?"

Dinah adjusted her cloak to cover her shoulder and raised her mantle over her head to cover her hair. "He was speaking the truth to you. He—he bothered to give you what he had left to give."

"But . . . but he is without God."

"You fool." Dinah shook her head. She looked up at her man. "There can be truth and goodness without God."

CHAPTER 26

Death

Azriel struggled for a shallow breath then gurgled throughout his final exhale.

Dinah stood helplessly and watched his face relax into eternity, watched the emptiness of forever wash over him, and watched his ugliness soften toward the formlessness of death.

A black bird landed on Azriel's shoulder and plucked out his good eye. Blood spattered on her face and on her mantle.

She did not have the strength to weep or to cry out against the black-winged world. She did not wipe off the blood.

She peered at Addan, who stood quietly nearby. "Your prophet, Jesus, did not die any better. And yet, nobody will be allowed to take my Azriel down from that cross. I am his woman. And I am truly nobody."

Addan took a careful step toward her and bowed his head respectfully. He could not, would not dare to speak.

"I do not like the women who follow your prophet, Jesus. But I respect their courage and determination. Some of them are not hypocrites." She extended her right hand and touched Azriel's left foot. "They accompanied your Master to the end. They took him from the cross with the intent to cleanse and anoint his body for a sepulcher. And they defied all the powers that our men have to offer us. I hope, for the sake of all women, and for all men, that they succeed. But they won't." She gazed up at Azriel's still body. "I wish he could curse at me one more time, the dear heart." She noted Addan's confusion. "Words. Toward me, his harsh words had no power." She almost smiled. "Only his deeds. His generous and gentle deeds toward me revealed his true nature." She extended her other hand and caressed both his bloody feet. She kissed his left ankle. She found strength to weep.

CHAPTER 27

Jesus

Addan was relieved to be free from that sorrowful woman who mourned for a criminal. He was frightened by her volatility and her unpredictability. But he was also sympathetic for her loss.

He watched her caress whatever she could reach of her man.

Her love was as genuine and as cleansing as love was capable of being.

Another black bird landed on the crossbeam that held Azriel's arm.

Addan turned away from Azriel and approached the foot of Jesus' empty cross. He bowed his head and prayed. "Nothing can separate me from you, Rabbi Jesus. You chose me, remember? You—you made me the example of innocence. And even though I have fallen from the grace of your caress these recent days, I know you have not stopped loving me." Addan dropped to his knees near the foot of the empty cross. "Jeshua was wrong when he said I could never go back after tasting the sweetness of evil. He was wrong because I have never left. I am still your servant because you won't let me be otherwise. I am not too late, because there is no late. Oh, God, my God who is beyond time and love and this place—Golgotha. Help me understand." Addan touched the rough wood of the upright stake and felt calmer. Clearer. Aware—of God's grace. "Am I crazy? I'm crazy. Yes, I know that. I . . . I'm speaking in tongues, I think. Because . . . because who can understand this . . . this—me. You always spoke of love no matter what. So. So. Here I am, Rabbi. No matter what, I stand before you. Convinced, I hope, that nothing can separate our love—no matter what." Addan pulled his hand away from the wood. "Nothing can make me forget your embrace before all men and your words to them as you continued to hold me in your arms: '*Whoever receives one child such as this in my name, receives me; and whoever receives me, receives not me but the one who sent me.*'" Tears streamed down his cheeks. "I believe I understand you now. I believe I understand loving God and loving all others. That's the Law. Through you, and from your embrace that day before my jealous father, there it was: all the Law. And God was present. God is present." Addan closed his eyes. "Help me, Lord. Choose to continue to be present. And—" Addan felt the weight of Jesus' right hand on his left shoulder and he felt the pain of the Roman legionnaire's whip after he stepped between them to protect his Jesus. "And yes, please—choose to give me the strength to face a present that I know will often be painful before there is any joy."

Addan was startled when Dinah touched his shoulder. "Ahh!"

The auxiliary garrison guards laughed.

"Did you not listen to what Azriel said to you? Your prophet is gone. There's no point in reaching up to the emptiness of the cross. Your prayers will be lost. We are all lost." She released his shoulder, frowned at him, then returned to the foot of Azriel's cross. Dinah knelt before Azriel and bowed her head. She appeared to be praying.

Addan did not care that the guards continued to laugh at him, at her, at them.

He suddenly decided that he was not going to be ashamed of what he believed in—even if he wasn't sure what that belief was yet. But he knew he would know what it was eventually if he continued to pray.

Addan raised his head and looked into the sky past the head of Jesus' cross and almost felt as if his emptiness had been filled, almost felt as if he had the spirit of God living inside him, the more he became closer to him—or so it felt, and so he hoped.

He was confused by these feelings, and embarrassed by their nakedness before God.

He suddenly felt comforted by his mourning. He suddenly felt released from the depths of his despair. He suddenly understood that everything was all right, even though he did not know how or why or what it was he understood or what he was all right about.

Addan studied the empty cross of Jesus. This implement of his rabbi's execution was no longer offensive or frightening. He knew Rabbi Jesus' spirit lived within him. And this . . . this spirit felt new.

Addan bowed his head.

He felt right with God.

He did not feel abandoned.

He closed his eyes and leaned against the foot of the cross. An overpowering exhaustion brought him to unconsciousness.

CHAPTER 28

Vision

He traveled along a main street cloaked in its predawn shadows. He traveled haphazardly toward an undecided destination, yet, he continued. He traveled invisibly.

Addan turned into a smaller street and stopped, not knowing how he had gotten there or where he was going next.

He felt the tap tap tap of heavy drops of rain. He squinted at the early morning light of sunrise. The orange disc near the horizon taunted him through this odd rain that came down in huge sparse drops. His burning eyes reminded him of his prayerful night on Golgotha. And yet, this daybreak felt new.

He saw the old woman who fed him yesterday. He saw Dinah, who embodied a different kind of love that wasn't different and, yet, without God, why was it not the same?

Addan saw more and more people the deeper he penetrated Jerusalem's lower quarter. People appeared to be the same to him. They were the same!

But he was not.

What was it that had changed? What had deepened within him?

His belief? His faith? His understanding? His love? Compassion?

Words. All words. None of them hit the mark, because there was no mark to hit.

Addan continued walking almost as if he were in a daze.

He did not feel alone.

How could that be? How could he feel a presence within him that was other than his own? How could he feel as if his own spirit were being supported by . . . by a greater spirit?

He was frightened, not because of the strange feeling he was experiencing, but because he was afraid that the feeling would stop. Or worse—that the feeling was an illusion.

Addan stopped walking. He tugged the front of his tunic with both hands for reassurance.

But it's not an illusion! It's not!

He started walking again and, shortly thereafter, he turned onto what appeared to be a smaller street, but was a back alley. Near its dead end, Addan saw two men crouched near a man who was sitting on the ground with his back pressed against the alley wall. They were engaged in a deep conversation.

As he carefully approached them, he recognized Peter first; then John. Addan was surprised by John's composure. He did not recognize the third man.

Addan crept as close as he could without drawing attention to himself, then crouched quietly.

He watched. He listened.

Peter was not doing all of the talking, but he was the one who spoke the loudest. "Don't look at me like I'm crazy."

Addan could not hear the following exchange between Peter and John until he heard John say, "It was Mary of Magdala and . . . and your own mother who saw that our Lord had risen."

Addan's face twitched.

By the cadence of his voice, Peter seemed disconnected. Addan heard Peter say, "Women," in a derogatory tone.

263

Peter leaned forward and rested his forearms against the thighs of his crossed legs. He appeared emotionally exhausted. He released a long sigh followed by a long convulsive sob. "He's risen from the dead. He's returned . . . I saw him. I felt the cold wound to one of his wrists. I . . . I."

John and the other man leaned closer to Peter.

Addan could not hear what they were saying, but that was all right. He knew that he, Peter, was speaking about Rabbi Jesus. That it was he who had risen. Risen. Was that what he had felt on Golgotha?

This rising. From within. Himself.

Addan was frightened.

How could he have experienced this rising without having known about it?

It's not possible. Or was it?

Addan struggled with himself to understand until he heard Peter shout: "He loved us all!"

The three men seemed to be arguing among themselves in the same manner that Addan was arguing with himself.

Peter leapt to his feet with excitement. "And he's bound to show himself to me, again."

It had stopped raining.

"You think so?" asked John.

Peter started walking toward the mouth of the alley. Addan flattened himself against the alley wall to get out of Peter's way.

"Where are you going?" John asked.

"To offer my humble prayers at the tomb of his resurrection." Peter walked past Addan without seeing him.

"Yes! Good," said John. "But . . . but then what?"

Peter stopped. He looked directly at Addan, but did not see him. Yet, it appeared as if he were speaking to Addan. "Then . . . then it's time to go back to fishing."

John and the other man caught up with Peter. Neither man noticed Addan.

Addan pressed his back and arms against the alley wall.

John stroked his bright red beard in dismay. "We haven't cast our nets in years."

"We have to eat." Peter turned to them. "So, I'll cast my nets until . . . until, well, until I hear his next call."

"Ah. Yes. *Follow me,*" John whispered.

"Yes. *Follow me.*" Peter's voice was clear and steady. Not like his glassy and shifty eyes that had frightened Addan into greater invisibility a moment ago. "Which one of us could ever forget the power of his *follow me*?" Peter turned away from John and the other man and began walking again.

"But wait!" said the other man.

"Yes, wait for us!" John shouted.

"I can't," said Peter. "I can no longer wait without the belief in his presence."

Together, the three of them approached the mouth of the back alley, turned to the right, and disappeared.

Addan stepped away from the wall as a witness to having seen and heard something important. Something that had changed him once again. No. Something that had verified what he had already felt—that he was new and . . . and renewed and . . . and now, visible—to himself.

He ran to the entrance of the back alley, not to follow these men who could not see him, but to orient himself on a busy Jerusalem street. He suddenly understood Rabbi Jesus' spirit and felt God's presence.

Addan stirred. He felt the foot of the cross against his left shoulder. He opened his eyes; he was awake. He hooked his right hand around the wood and rose to his feet. He shook his head.

He felt reborn and, yet, the same. Always the same.

He had to find his mother and his sisters and his brother and, yes, his father.

CHAPTER 29

Love

Addan passed through one of the gates that led into the lower quarter of Jerusalem, just before dawn when the lower gates were unlocked in anticipation of traffic greater than what their needle-eyes could handle.

The world seemed less gray. Less threatening. Less barbaric after his night on Golgotha.

As Addan traveled through Jerusalem's streets in search of his family and friends, he saw Jeshua's eyes, heard Jeshua's voice, felt Jeshua's evil disposition embodied in numerous people in the growing traffic and realized that evil was always not far from him and, therefore, evil was everywhere—waiting for him to fall, waiting for him to . . .

He saw his mother and his sisters and his brother in the distance. He saw them all as if for the first time in his life.

He approached them and immediately hugged his older sister. Their formal embrace, filled with love and respect, was all that was necessary between them.

"Where are you?" Addan's mother finally demanded. She looked into the altered seriousness of his eyes and realized he was no longer a boy. "And where have you been?"

"I've been lost," said Addan.

His mother nodded to convey her approval. "And now—? Now you are found."

He hugged his mother and whispered loud enough for his older sister to hear. "Now. Now I am here."

D. S. Lliteras is the author of nine critically acclaimed novels and one book of haiku and photography. He resides in Virginia Beach, Virginia, with his wife, Kathleen.

HAMPTON ROADS
PUBLISHING COMPANY, INC.

Thank you for reading *The Master of Secrets*. Hampton Roads is proud to publish the complete novels of D. S. Lliteras as well as other works of biblical fiction. Please take a look at the following selection or visit us anytime on the web: www.hrpub.com.

THE BIBLICAL NOVELS OF D. S. LLITERAS:

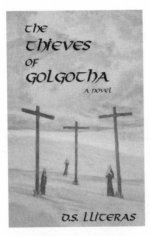

Hardcover • 192 pages
ISBN 1-57174-085-6 • $19.95

The Thieves of Golgotha
This dramatic portrayal of the two thieves who were crucified alongside Jesus will forever alter your interpretation of the crucifixion and your understanding of Jesus.

"Thought-provoking.
Recommended."
—*Library Journal*

Hardcover • 240 pages
ISBN 1-57174-144-5 • $19.95

Judas the Gentile

This follow-up to *The Thieves of Golgotha* explores the conflict between human desires and our destiny. Lliteras artfully sifts through two thousand years of myth to reveal the complexities of the true Judas and his intricate relationship with Jesus.

"Top 10 Christian Novel of 2000. Subtle, provocative."
—*Booklist*

Hardcover • 232 pages
ISBN 1-57174-340-5 • $19.95

Jerusalem's Rain

Lliteras depicts Peter and Jesus' other disciples who remain in the city following the Crucifixion. Peter, struggling with his master's death and his own denial of Jesus, sinks into the depths of despair. At his lowest point he is met by the resurrected Christ who greets him with love and the renewal of his stirring call: "Follow me."

Jerusalem's Rain (cont.)

"Top 10 Christian Novel of 2003.
Lliteras' great achievement."
—*Booklist*

"Best Genre Fiction of 2003.
Outstanding biblical novel."
—*Library Journal*

Hardcover • 256 pages
ISBN 1-57174-410-X • $19.95

The Silence of John

"The Silence of the Apostle John during the crucifixion of Jesus sets the stage for another outstanding effort. . . . Lliteras's emotionally charged account examines in painstaking detail their early influence and later suppression in church leadership. His ability to turn historical figures into living, breathing human beings and a fast-paced plot make this New Testament depiction a highly recommended purchase."—*Library Journal*

In the Heart of Things

Stranded on the streets of Baltimore, Llewellen has lost everything that provided him with identity. At his lowest point, he encounters Jansen, an American Zen master, and discovers that enlightened living is possible for anyone, anywhere.

Paperback • 176 pages • ISBN 1-878901-22-2
$8.95

Into the Ashes

Llewellen returns home and realizes the difficulty of living on the path. Somehow, he must discover the reality of his experience with Jansen to fully comprehend what he has learned.

Paperback • 208 pages • ISBN 1-878901-77-X
$9.95

Half-Hidden by Twilight

"Escaping into life," Llewellen discovers that the challenges of human existence are the gateways to love, understanding, and being yourself.

Paperback • 176 pages • ISBN 1-57174-000-7
$9.95

Hampton Roads Publishing Company

. . . for the evolving human spirit

Hampton Roads Publishing Company
publishes books on a variety of subjects,
including metaphysics, spirituality,
health, visionary fiction, and other related topics.

For a copy of our latest trade catalog,
call toll-free, 800-766-8009,
or send your name and address to:

Hampton Roads Publishing Company, Inc.
1125 Stoney Ridge Road
Charlottesville, VA 22902
E-mail: hrpc@hrpub.com
Internet: www.hrpub.com